Captured Hearts

Captured Hearts

MARY CATHERINE HANSON

DOUBLEDAY & COMPANY, INC.

GARDEN CITY, NEW YORK

1982

To my mother and father,
Sarah and Jack

All of the characters in this book
are fictitious, and any resemblance
to actual persons, living or dead,
is purely coincidental.

First Edition

ISBN: 0-385-17827-1
Library of Congress Catalog Card Number 81–43651
Printed in the United States of America

Captured Hearts

MARY CATHERINE HANSON

DOUBLEDAY & COMPANY, INC.

GARDEN CITY, NEW YORK

1982

To my mother and father,
Sarah and Jack

All of the characters in this book
are fictitious, and any resemblance
to actual persons, living or dead,
is purely coincidental.

First Edition

ISBN: 0-385-17827-1
Library of Congress Catalog Card Number 81–43651
Printed in the United States of America

CHAPTER 1

The heat of August had rolled away like a prickly fog, leaving in its wake high blue skies and crystal days that seemed to have suddenly arrived on zephyr winds, vanquishing the slow lazy pace of summer. Footsteps picked up and were light and brisk. Now each of the populace moved with vigor and purpose; their minds were set to pick up where spring had left off.

Metal shutters were raised from shopwindows that had not seen the light of day for more than a month; the city was no longer left to old newspapers drifting along aimlessly on hot currents of air down deserted streets. Rome, who sleeps in the summer as a bear sleeps in winter, was awakening to a new season. September had arrived.

The salmon-pink twilight sky that seems indigenous to Italy melted into an indigo blue, introducing the evening breeze that flowed lightly through the French doors from the terrace of Adelaide Huxley's apartment, billowing thin silk white curtains in its path. Through the opened windows the apartment glowed in the soft light of an overhead chandelier that cast in its light the glitter of a small gathering of very elegantly dressed men and women, who were the vanguard of the returning legions who had fled Rome's heat for the coolness of the countryside and the seashore.

In one circle Adelaide stood resplendent in a gown of sapphire blue, with diamonds and sapphires splattering dazzling spears of light from the necklace around her throat.

Adelaide Huxley was a very rich woman. She had houses and apartments in major cities about the world. She was not thought of as an empty jet setter; she was a woman of means with a purpose in life, which her money enabled her to accomplish. Adelaide was a patron of the arts. She herself had not one iota of artistic ability, so she made up for her lack of creativity by helping those who were gifted, and she worked with incredibly unyielding vigor to bring as much beauty to the world as was in her power, which was considerable.

Tonight, Adelaide was hostess to a small select group of musicians, writers, painters, and an actor or two, in celebration of a young pianist who had just won the coveted Tchaikovsky Award in Moscow. The pianist sat uncomfortably in a small group of well-wishers who wanted to know of his plans for the future, and simply to know something about him. With so much attention centered on him, the young man found it difficult to relax, and he found himself unconsciously twining his long graceful fingers in and out of each other. He spoke only when asked a direct question, and then words did not come easy; but he was beginning to discover that the people who were gathered here tonight were far from pretentious snobs with false aloofness that the young man had thought they might have developed with their world-renowned success. Instead, he found them a congenial bunch who used risqué language and laughed at each other's corny jokes, and had a deep compassion for life with its ups and downs. But he still had a hard time making himself believe that these people were here tonight to celebrate him, and he went on twining his fingers in and out of each other.

Adelaide pranced over to join the small group that contained her guest of honor.

"Does anyone need anything here?" She smiled at them through ruby lips, flashing beautiful white teeth as she brushed back an imaginary stray strand into her magnificently styled dark hair. Her face glowed with tinges of pink radiating from her cheeks. Clearly, the evening and the company had fanned the fires of Adelaide's spirit. She was very pleased tonight with her introduction of—she was certain—a fine new talent to her friends.

She perched herself gracefully on the arm of the chair of the young man and searched the group for a moment.

"Other than a lady or two, there are some lovely ones here tonight." Adelaide interrupted herself when a woman appeared in the doorway. She waved until she got the woman's attention. She started to move toward Adelaide, stopping on the way to greet some of the guests. When she finally reached Adelaide, she leaned over and kissed her lightly on both cheeks.

"Sorry I'm late, Adelaide. It's this awful last-minute packing." The men stood up to greet her, all of whom she knew except for the guest of honor, who stood, awkwardly stumbling against the leg of his chair. Adelaide rose and said, "Nonsense. I'm glad you've come, darling." She took the hand of the woman like a schoolgirl.

"You must meet our new musical genius. Anais, let me present Gathen Bentley."

The young man took the extended hand of the woman and looked down into the loveliest face that he had ever seen. Dark smoky hair hung just to her shoulders, framing a silky golden face. She smiled at him with eyes of sparkling topaz fringed with thick black lashes. A large silk flower blossomed on the shoulder of her gown, and she glowed like a golden pearl. She said, "Hello," and her voice sounded to Gathen like musical wind chimes tinkling in the crystal air of a Tibetan mountain.

With a feeling of urgency, Gathen offered his chair to this beautiful woman. He could not let her wander away and join some of the other guests. Gathen breathed an inward sigh of relief when Anais accepted his seat. He immediately took a place on the floor beside her. He watched her with fascination as she leaned gracefully back against the silk down cushion of the French chair and prepared to join in the conversation.

Through the blue haze of transparent smoke, the tinkling crystal glasses filled with fine liqueurs, and the buzz of good conversation, the party was coming to an end. Groups had interchanged many times during the course of the evening, but Anais and Gathen had remained in their same place throughout the evening. Gathen had scarcely taken his eyes off Anais. Only when she felt his steady gaze and turned to look at him did he lower his eyes and look away.

Adelaide joined them again after mingling most of the evening with all of her guests. Though the hour was late, she was still aglow, not showing the least sign of fatigue. She raised her hand again to brush the imagined stray hair back. She laughed gaily and said, "I don't know when I've

had such a marvelous evening." Adelaide did not comment on Anais and Gathen's not having circulated among the guests, but she had noticed.

Anais glanced at the watch of one of the guests and exclaimed, "Oh, dear, I didn't realize it was so late. I must leave now."

"Surely, Anais, you are not planning to go home tonight. Stay and we can have a long talk over breakfast in the morning," Adelaide coaxed. She looked at the same watch and said, "Well, later on this morning."

"Thank you, Adelaide, but I still have a lot of packing left to do, and I had better get to it as soon as possible."

"Well, you certainly can't go home alone." She looked at Gathen and said, "Anais doesn't live far from here. Would you see her safely home?" Gathen smiled broadly at both of them and replied, "I'd love to."

"You're very kind. I'll get my things," Anais said, hurrying off. She was back in a few moments.

"I'm ready. Thank you, Adelaide, for a lovely evening. I'll call you tomorrow."

Gathen took both of Adelaide's hands and clasped them in his elegant fingers and said soberly, "How can I ever thank you?"

"You have: you came." And Adelaide stood on her tiptoes to reach his face and kissed him on both cheeks, a European custom that she and Anais had adopted with their years of travel. They spoke of telephoning and said good night.

CHAPTER 2

In a few minutes, Anais and Gathen were down on the deserted street. Their footsteps were hollow as they echoed against the silence of the night. The yellow light of the streetlamps glowed up into the trees and turned their tired dusty leaves into a spring green. The night was beautiful and deceiving, and it seemed more like the beginning of spring than the start of autumn with winter soon to come.

On this balmy deceptive September night, the illusion of spring played in the head of Gathen Bentley, and without thought of consequences and with complete abandon, he fell in love with the beautiful woman who walked beside him. His heart could not see that the leaves were straining to pull away from their branches, and some already lay decaying along the gutter. It was not spring after all.

Anais and Gathen strolled along the deserted street toward the Via Veneto, laughing and talking softly. They soon came upon a carriage with a sleepy driver, whose head rested low on his chest, and a sad-looking old horse that stood as still as a statue. As they drew near, the driver suddenly breathed life and, with a wide scatter-toothed grin, chanted at them, "Carriage! Carriage, signore?"

"Hey! This is living," Gathen said as he guided Anais toward the carriage. He helped her into the seat and climbed in beside her. The driver clicked his teeth and the carriage moved slowly away from the curb. The driver turned to them for directions. Gathen looked at Anais and said, "Let's just ride around for a while."

"All right," Anais said with a slight hesitation in her voice.

Anais told the driver in Italian, and he nodded his head. Neither of them spoke. Anais finally thought of something to say to break the silence that was becoming too comfortable, and she asked, "How long will you be in Rome?"

"I don't know, perhaps another month. And you?"

"I leave next week," she replied.

"So soon?" he said with disappointment in his voice.

"My family's already left. I stayed behind to close the apartment and the house in the country. We spend all of our summers in Italy. We come in May and stay until September. In July we flee Rome and go to the house in the country. Rome is unbearably hot in August." Anais smiled at Gathen.

"How long have you been coming to Italy?" Gathen asked.

"Well, my parents traveled to Europe a great deal before the war, when Europe was so gay and dazzling to Americans. During the war my father was stationed here and fell in love with the country and could hardly wait to bring Mother back and share it with her. I came along. We've been coming back ever since."

"Did you meet Adelaide here?"

"No. Adelaide and I went to school together. We have become quite close through the years. We've done almost everything together. One summer she came to Italy with us, and that was the beginning of our true love affair with

Italy. We did so many things that summer that we had never done before that we begged to stay on afterward." Anais spread the palms of her hands upward.

"My poor father and hers couldn't stand our begging another moment and gave in just for the sake of a few moments without tears." Anais laughed at the memory of those days. "Later, my father bought the apartment from the old contessa that we were renting from and gave it to me as a birthday present. And here we are, still." She inclined her head slightly with a questioning smile.

"I know I'm staring at you. I was just thinking what a beautiful lady you are."

She did not acknowledge his compliment except for a faint smile, and Gathen thought, "She knows it." He was used to girls blushing and looking demure when he told them that they were pretty, but he liked this, yes, he liked this very much indeed.

They were now driving along the Avenue of the Magnolias in the gardens of the Villa Borghese. The trees, stirring in the warm breeze, whispered to each other in the darkness. Looking up into the trees, Anais said, "Oh, I love magnolias. I wish they were in bloom now."

"So do I," Gathen said.

"Oh, do you like magnolias, too?"

"Not particularly. There are a lot of them where I come from. But if they were in bloom now, I would climb the nearest tree and pick a bunch and lay them at your feet."

The eyes that burned with the expectation of youth, that always seemed to be looking just to the next horizon, took focus and looked deep into Anais' eyes. Anais became uncomfortable under Gathen's steady gaze and said,

"I must go home now or I will never be able to get up in the morning. There is so much to do. It makes me weak just thinking about it."

"All right, but you had better give the driver your address. My Italian isn't what it should be."

Anais leaned forward and said, *"Dodici Via Bon Compagne, per piacere."* They settled back against the comfortable old worn leather seats for the last of the ride.

Gathen clasped his hands behind his head and looked up into the clear dark-blue sky that was dotted with a myriad of twinkling stars. His thoughts were now traveling to join them.

It was Anais' turn to peer at the young man sitting next to her with secretive eyes. She thought him confident and innocent. His features were strong but sensitive, a face that certainly appealed to women. His soft brown hair was thick and had just one wave at the end where it was cut and it flipped romantically up. His dark brows cast a shadow over his chestnut-brown eyes, and his expression was now that of a child, innocent and at peace with the world. He turned to look at her for a moment and their eyes locked in desire. Then he returned to gazing at the stars. Anais smiled to herself and thought, "You won't have to wait, Gathen. You will have success and it will continue long after your youth has faded."

"It's all written in the stars," she said and looked at him, and he looked at her with a puzzled stare.

The carriage rolled to a stop and jolted Gathen out of his perplexity.

"We're here," Anais said.

Gathen jumped from the carriage and took both of

Anais' hands as she stepped down from the carriage. The warmth of his touch made her feel as if she were descending suddenly in an elevator, and a flush of pink rose in her cheeks at this absurdity.

The magnificent black mahogany doors with their regal brass knockers were locked for the night, and Anais had to search through her small silk purse for the keys. She came up with a large brass key that fitted into the large keyhole. Gathen unlocked the door and made a gesture for the driver to wait.

They entered a white marbled lobby where large terra-cotta pots, filled with green plants, encircled the white floor. A lacy wrought-iron railing curved gracefully up to each landing, and in the middle of the floor sat a tiny lift. Gathen pressed the button and the gate sprang open with a clang. Anais pressed the top button, and with a sharp start they ascended, like splendid birds in a cage.

They stood quite close to each other because of the smallness of the lift, and they were so conscious of each other that neither of them dared to speak. The lift came to a bumpy stop, and they stepped out onto a narrow landing which led up to gleaming white steps that stopped at two beautiful black lacquered doors with shining brass knockers, a smaller reproduction of the doors in the lobby. Gathen opened one of the doors and returned the key to Anais. She offered her hand and said, "You've been very kind."

"Not at all. It's been my pleasure." He took her hand and pressed it to his lips, and not knowing what else to do he said good night and bounded down the steps to the waiting lift.

Anais closed the door quickly and ran to the terrace to watch Gathen emerge from the building. He came out shortly. The streetlamp, highlighting his hair, cast his face in shadows. Anais hung over the terrace giggling like a schoolgirl as the breeze played with her hair. She even burst out with a laugh as Gathen made futile gestures with his hands. Finally he gave up and took a piece of paper from his pocket, wrote on it, and handed it to the driver, who bobbed his head up and down. He climbed into the carriage, and it moved slowly away with its sad horse, its sleepy driver, and Gathen, disappearing under the dark trees.

For the life of her, Anais could not imagine why she had gone to the terrace to watch Gathen leave, and why did she feel suddenly lonely?

CHAPTER 3

The night was not a restful one for Anais. Small details of unimportant things kept running through her mind; these little annoyances did nothing to dispel the pleasantness of the evening, though. She remembered that the carriage ride had been the nicest part of the evening. She pushed herself up in bed and rested against the headboard and tried to put her finger on what was bothering her. The uneasiness still lurked in the shadows of her mind as she drifted off to sleep.

Anais was awakened by the ringing of the telephone. She listened in the darkness of her room as Pina's house shoes shuffled across the marble floor. Pina's voice traveled through the closed door.

"*Pronto*." A pause while the other party spoke. "I'll see, signore."

In the dimness of the room Anais saw Pina's head peek around the door.

"Signorina," the little maid whispered.

"Yes, Pina. I'm awake. Who is it?"

"A Signor Bentley."

"Oh!" Anais quickly flung the covers back and put her dressing gown on. She combed her hair back with her fingers as she hurried to the telephone, which sat on an ornately carved chest in the foyer. She picked up the receiver, trying very hard not to sound breathless.

"Hello, Gathen. My, you are up early." She was still combing her hair with her fingers as she smiled happily into the receiver. Gathen's voice came through the phone in high spirits.

"Have you seen what kind of day this is?" he asked.

"No, not yet. What kind of day is it?" She played the game with him as she tried to peer around the corner into a room where the drapes were opened.

"Well, it's one of those absolutely beautiful, great-to-be-alive days, and not to be wasted. So what do you say to having lunch somewhere in the country?"

Anais did not reply right away, and Gathen's voice came over the phone again.

"Humm, what do I hear?"

With much packing left to do, Anais knew that she should say no, but she laughed and heard herself saying, "What a lovely idea. I'll tell you what. I have to go to the house in the country, so why don't we have lunch there? It's only an hour and a half from Rome. It's a little place called Anticcolli, and I won't feel so guilty not getting my packing done."

"Okay. It is now"—Anais could tell that he was checking his watch—"nine o'clock. I have Wells's car, and I'll pick you up at ten-thirty. Is that all right?"

"All right, but I will have to hurry."

"Right, see you then." And he was gone.

Anais called to Pina. "Pina, would you run a bath for me, please?" She hurried to her room, swung open the closet door, and began pushing dresses and skirts aside. She decided on a soft white cotton dress with a full skirt and a pair of apricot sandals from the closet floor; on second thought she took out an apricot cashmere sweater, in case it became chilly later on in the day. Everything was laid out on the bed when Pina came to announce that her bath was ready.

"What would you like for breakfast, signorina?" Pina asked.

"No breakfast, Pina. I don't have time."

"No breakfast? But it is breakfast time."

Anais closed the bathroom door on Pina's protest. She slipped into the warm water and bathed quickly. By ten-fifteen she was fastening a strand of coral beads around her throat; small coral earrings already dotted her pierced ears. Anais carefully removed the emerald-cut diamond ring that circled her left-hand ring finger and placed it in her jewel box.

She gathered her things from the bed and was going to the foyer when she heard the knocker sound at the door. Pina went to the door, and to Anais' dismay her heart began to pound.

"How silly," she thought as she touched her chest. She listened as Pina greeted Gathen, and she heard him say, "I'm Gathen Bentley."

"Come in, signore. I will tell the signorina that you are here."

Anais appeared in the doorway just as Pina turned to fetch her.

"Good morning, Gathen." His eyes brightened when he

saw Anais. Their eyes fixed for a second, there was a look of tenderness, which betrayed an awakening desire. He smiled and said, "Ready?"

White morning sunshine flooded the street, and Anais was momentarily blinded as they emerged from the building. She shaded her eyes from the sun. "It is a glorious day."

"The car is over there." Gathen pointed to a silver Mercedes parked next to the American Embassy.

"I borrowed it from Wells. He has two cars, so it doesn't matter when we get it back." He opened the door for her and then got in on the other side. He turned the ignition key and the engine turned over and purred. He said, "Which way do we go?"

"Turn left at Via Veneto. We will stay on that for a while, and then I will tell you which turn to take at the circle."

They soon came to a cobbled circle and Anais directed Gathen again and they headed out of Rome. The car glided over the country road, and they felt the rapture of the soft country air that filled their lungs through the open windows. Umbrella and cypress trees dotted the landscape like a Renaissance painting while farmers went about their daily work, and the farm animals grazed along the hillside, taking little note of their romantic setting or of the sleek silver car that sped by them.

Anais touched Gathen's arm and exclaimed, "Oh, look, Gathen. There's the Villa d'Este. Let's stop for a moment."

"Great. I've always wanted to see it," he said, slowing the car down and pulling into a parking area. They walked to the entrance, where the fee was a few liras.

They walked outside again and stood at the top of high sweeping steps that looked down on the magnificent fountains coursing in a glittering silver arch with bright rainbows shining in the misty spray that scattered in the wind. Gathen was so taken with the beauty of the place that he could only smile broadly. They walked down the expansive steps to the fountains. Anais told Gathen the story of the mischievous cardinal who would invite visitors to see the garden, then excuse himself, go inside and turn the fountains on them. They both laughed at the thought of soaking-wet dignitaries.

"I'll bet they had a few unholy names for His Eminence." Gathen chuckled again at the thought.

They spent a little more time in the gardens, then in the museum, often glancing at each other when they thought the other was not aware. They finished the villa and started on their way again.

The miles slipped away while they exchanged small confidences of likes and dislikes. They smiled at each other a lot, with glances that met and held now, as they became more and more aware of the growing subtle feeling of harmony that was unfolding between them.

Everything enchanted them.

"Isn't it beautiful, Gathen?"

"What?" he asked.

"The olive grove," she answered as she turned to watch the trees as they passed. The soft country air stirred the leaves to a mass of shimmering silver.

"It's going to rain." Gathen looked at Anais in surprise as his eyes swept across the blue sky. He turned the corners of his mouth down and said, "Impossible."

"Well, there's a saying that when the wind blows the leaves of the olive trees so that their silver underside shows, it means that it will rain." Gathen smiled at her as though she were a child.

"I'm sure it will again one day. But not today. Of course, not to disavow an old folktale, just not today." He smiled again at her.

"I hope that you are right." Anais smiled back at him. She leaned her head back against the red leather seat, then sat up suddenly.

"We turn off soon. You will see two stone pillars. We turn in there. They came shortly to the pillars, which sat on either side of a gravel road. Gathen drove slowly up the road, which was not very smooth. A peasant woman strode along the side of the road carrying a basket on her head. Anais waved to the woman as Gathen slowed to pass her. The woman turned to see who was in the car, and Gathen saw remnants of great beauty. The woman's skin was leathery and wrinkled; black shiny hair mixed with gray strayed from beneath the black scarf that she wore on her head. Her smile showed teeth that were decaying from lack of attention. But time and toil had not touched the magnificent brown eyes. Anais read Gathen's thoughts as he looked at the woman.

"It's too much sun and too much hard work. It takes its toll."

"She must have been very beautiful," he said thoughtfully.

"Yes," Anais said with compassion.

The villa stood in a circle drive that wound itself from the little gravel road. The house was comfortably large.

The roof was flat, with stone balustrades going completely around the top. The sand-colored walls were dotted with white-trimmed paned windows, and two French doors opened onto a balcony on the upper floor. The terrace on the first floor stretched across the entire front of the villa, and wide stone balustraded steps divided the terrace in the center, which led up to two pickled-walnut doors, and on each side French doors spanned the terrace.

A curtain of dark-green trees waved behind the villa, highlighting it as a thing of solid beauty. The garden was terraced and part of it sloped down to touch the roof of the kitchen. It then fanned out and continued its incline down to a long reflecting pool, which mirrored back white and yellow chrysanthemums and late-blooming roses against the azure sky.

Just under the terrace a little fountain with a slim stem of water cascaded into a calla lily before spilling back into its pool.

"What a beautiful place," Gathen said in admiration.

"This is my mother's house. She got the house and I got the apartment. Both birthday presents. So we share them." Anais laughed lightly.

"That's nice," Gathen said, in awe of such splendor.

Just as they reached the top of the steps the door opened and a pretty girl with peaches-and-cream skin greeted them.

"Signorina." She smiled sweetly as she stood aside to let them enter. She closed the door and followed behind them. Anais turned to her and said, "Victoria, this is Gathen Bentley."

CHAPTER 4

When Gathen trotted down the steps, he met Anais in the hall and she led him into the drawing room. The room was born of a past era, when elegance reigned. The ceiling was high with carved rosettes in the center. The furniture was in the style of Louis XV, and the walls were of a creamy eggshell. Paintings, large and small, decorated the walls, and a large tapestry of knights with their fair maidens hung from one surface. A garland-carved fireplace of creamy beige marble was laid with dark logs behind a brass fan fire screen, and in the corner near the French doors, a dark gleaming grand piano sat majestically in the shadows. Through the opened door, a breeze played softly with the curtains, where a table was set with beautiful china and crystal that reflected the afternoon light from their rich delicate surfaces. A dark-green wine bottle stood above the setting. Prosciutto and melon were already on the first plates.

"That looks good," Gathen said as he held Anais' chair. They were both seated and fell into easy light conversation.

"Tell me about yourself," Anais said.

"What would you like to know?" Gathen gave her a teasing smile.

Anais cocked her head to one side. "Well, first, where are you from?"

"I'm from a small town in South Carolina called Harrods. Let me see," he pondered teasingly. "I went to high school there, and I had a piano teacher who thought she saw more in me than her average protesting students. So when I graduated, she had already written to Juilliard. My father took me to New York for the audition and here I am, having lunch with you, in the country in Italy, and all because of my high school teacher." He smiled at her.

"Surely you did not protest your music lessons," Anais said.

"Every step of the way." Gathen laughed.

Anais rested her chin in her hands and continued her interrogation of Gathen.

"How did you meet Adelaide?"

"Through Wells Phipps. Do you know him?"

"Yes, for many years," she answered. Anais sat quietly watching Gathen, and he reached over and flicked the tip of her nose with his forefinger.

"What are you thinking about?" Gathen asked her playfully.

"Nothing, really." Anais giggled suddenly. "I'm always silly when I drink wine at lunch."

"Good. I like silly women," he said.

"Everyone will rest after lunch. Would you like to rest or go for a walk?" Anais asked.

"I think I'll opt for a walk. I'm stuffed," Gathen groaned.

As they walked through the French doors onto the terrace that was lined with clay pots filled with red geraniums, they paused for a moment to watch Alberto, the gardener, putting the finishing touches on the lawn he had just mowed. They observed Alberto silently as he scooped up the freshly cut grass and put it into a wheelbarrow; the fragrance meandered up to reach them on the terrace.

"Hmm-mm, that smells good," Gathen said. From behind them Victoria spoke softly.

"*Signorina*, may I have a word with you for a moment, please?"

"Of course, Victoria. I'll be along in a moment, Gathen."

Victoria's brows were creased with a worried frown as Anais followed her back through the French doors. Victoria turned and said, "Angelina's nephew is here with a message from her. He says that Angelina has not finished your mother's dress, but it will be ready first thing tomorrow morning."

"Oh, my, this is a problem. Tell the boy to tell Angelina that I'll let her know later on this afternoon what I'll do about the dress."

Gathen had joined Alberto, and Alberto was chuckling softly as Gathen looked a little sheepish. "I just told Alberto that he cut the hair of the grass beautifully."

A chuckle rose in Anais' throat, then a laugh burst forth. She put her hand to her mouth and said, "I'm sorry, Gathen." She couldn't stop laughing.

"I can see that I'm going to have to do something about my Italian," he said, grinning. "And you are not to make fun of me."

"Really, Gathen, the hair of the grass."

They waved good-bye to Alberto, who was still smiling

at Gathen, and started on their walk. They soon came upon a narrow path that led into the woods. Grasshoppers jumped in front of them with wisps of their wings crying against the silence, and birds fluttered from branch to branch as Anais and Gathen intruded upon their sanctuary. They followed the path deeper into the woods where there was little sunlight and the air was cool and moist. The ground was covered with a thick green velvet carpet of moss. Anais suddenly slipped on the moss and Gathen put his arm around her waist to steady her, and again the wild beating of her heart made her giddy and light-headed —so much so that she thought that surely she would faint.

"All right?" she heard him say.

"Yes. I'm all right." She managed a smile, but her soul was traveling on a desperate road to Gathen and was now out of control with love, and indeed she was not all right.

They came to a clearing in the woods and stood on a gentle sloping hill that looked down into a valley and over an old hill town that sat stately against a russet earth spotted with greenery.

"We can sit here for a while," Anais said, pointing to a large gray stone protruding from the ground. Anais said thoughtfully, "Hill towns look so beautiful from a distance, but when you get up to them, they are old and decaying and the women sit in front of the doorways sewing and crocheting all day. I suppose just not to be inside those dark musty old houses." Anais sighed. "I suppose there are many things that are not what they seem."

She stared out over the valley for a few moments. Then suddenly remembering her mother's dress, she said, "Gathen, I don't know what to do about my mother's dress. I came down to get it and her dressmaker has sent word that it won't be ready until tomorrow morning. I don't want to leave it. She has her heart set on wearing it to one of her whatevers."

"Well, if it's all right with you, we can stay the night and drive back tomorrow," he said.

"Oh, Gathen, I don't want to keep you if you have other plans," she said.

"I don't have any plans, and Wells doesn't need the car. He's out of town anyway."

"Oh, good. Mother would die if I left without it."

"That's settled. Shall we go back now?"

"No, not yet. I want you to see the little train that appears every afternoon at four o'clock and then disappears again."

They waited a few moments and sure enough a little black engine came chugging from nowhere. The rhythm of its engine and wheels rose up from the ravine and held them captive for a moment and then it was gone.

"It looks like something I used to play with." Gathen grinned.

They arrived back at the villa, tired and silent, occupied with their own thoughts. They entered the sitting room through the French doors; there was no one about now, and the room was still except for the gentle billowing of the silk curtains at the doors.

"Would you like to rest for a while?" Anais asked.

"No, let's just sit here and talk for a bit," he replied.

Gathen noticed a guitar sitting in the corner next to the piano. He went over and picked it up.

"Would you like to play the piano?"

"No," he answered, testing the strings of the guitar to see if it was tuned. He adjusted some of the strings and sat down on the sofa next to Anais and began to play the guitar.

The sky was a delicate mauve, streaked with gold from the last rays of the setting sun, and twilight stole softly into the room while the strings of the guitar filled it with the strains of an old love song, "Ramona."

Anais listened, enraptured by the beauty of the sounds that came from an instrument that had always just had its strings plucked for a second and then sat unappreciated back into the corner again. Until now she had not realized the magnitude of beauty that had been bestowed upon this conveyance of the angels.

When Gathen had finished playing, he looked deep into Anais' golden eyes that were half hidden in the shadows of dusk, and said softly, "I bless the day you taught me to care." Gathen put the guitar down beside the sofa and leaned back against the cushions and closed his eyes, as if suddenly his energies were spent.

"You are tired," Anais said with compassion.

"A bit. It's quiet and peaceful here," he replied without opening his eyes.

Anais studied his face for a moment and said, "Shall we go to our rooms and rest before dinner?"

At eight o'clock they came downstairs. Anais had changed into a soft silk dress of pale apricot that fluttered around her like a butterfly. She looked fresh and bright as she greeted Gathen on the stairs.

"You look lovely," he said, "but that's not fair: you've changed."

Anais laughed liltingly and pointed to her sandals. "Same shoes."

Gathen looked equally refreshed. He had put his jacket and tie back on for dinner. His hair was still damp from the shower and was beginning to fall free from its careful combing.

They beheld each other with admiration.

Victoria appeared at the bottom of the stairs and after a few moments managed to get their attention to announce that dinner was served.

The dining room danced in the flickering yellow light of candles and the crystal wineglasses glittered as they were touched by the glow of the flames. The table was set for two: one place at the head and the other at the right. Anais stepped to the chair at the side and for a moment Gathen was confused, but he held the chair for Anais and then took the seat at the head of the table.

Dinner was delightful. The old wine was excellent and set a mellowing mood. Their conversation was relaxed and amusing with playful bantering between them. As dinner came to a close, they sat with elbows on the table sipping wine. Their conversation slipped into silence. Anais tilted her head slightly to one side and stared dreamily into the flame of the candles. Gathen spoke to her.

"Come back to me, Anais. Wherever it is that you have wandered, it makes you sad," he said.

Anais leaned back against her chair; she smiled at him with eyes that were too bright and said, "The wine seems to have a different effect in candlelight."

For a moment Gathen thought he saw tears swim in her eyes, but she quickly shielded them with her hand for a second. When she removed her hand, her eyes were only sparkling in the flickering light. She smiled at him again and said, "I didn't know that you played the guitar."

He winked at her mischievously and said, "You're going to have to stick close to me, kid, so that you can find out all the things that I can do." He glanced at the clock on the mantel as it struck eleven. Anais' eyes followed his glance to the clock.

"Is it your bedtime?" he asked.

Anais thought for a moment. "Well, I suppose we will have to get an early start in the morning, and Adelaide is no doubt wondering what has become of us."

They turned the lights out and walked slowly up the stairs. Gathen's room was next to Anais'. He said good night to her at her door. He kissed the tips of her fingers lightly, and they both found the moment disturbing. So, without lingering, Anais entered her room.

Anais undressed slowly, pacing around the room as she shed each garment, stopping to stare at objects with deep thought as she fingered them without really seeing them. After about an hour of abstract thoughts, Anais finally had her nightgown on. The touch of the pale-turquoise satin was like a cooling balm to her warm flesh, and the marble floor chilled her bare feet.

Anais lay down in the middle of her bed and traced the shadows on the ceiling. Unable to close her eyes, Anais slipped into her dressing gown and walked onto the balcony in her bare feet. She leaned against the railing and searched the inky blue sky and breathed in the calm night air.

The stars twinkled in the heavens with the ice-blue flame of a million diamonds strewn across a dark sea of velvet.

"Well, good evening."

"Oh!" Anais jumped at the sound of Gathen's voice.

"Couldn't sleep either?" he asked.

"No," she admitted. "I'm a bit wound up, I suppose." She smiled at him in the shadows of the trees that moved gently across her face.

Gathen had not undressed; he had removed his jacket though, and his shirt was unbuttoned at the collar with the cuffs turned up almost to his elbows. He seemed restless to Anais, but he only said, "I thought I heard someone walking under the window."

Anais laughed and leaned over the balustrade. She beckoned Gathen to lean over with her.

"Listen," she said. "It's the fountain. When we first moved here someone was up every night looking for a culprit, until Alberto told us that it was the fountain. Can you hear the pattering of feet?"

"Yes. Funny." They leaned over the railing together listening silently to the silver stream of water that rushed up to them.

Gathen broke the silence with words that sent shivers through Anais' body. He whispered through her dark hair that played around his face.

"I love you, Anais. I have, I believe, from the moment you walked through the door at Adelaide's," he said as he gently brushed her hair back from her face.

Anais wanted to protest, but her body responded to the declaration and she floated into his arms. He took her ever so gently, enfolding her in his arms. He stroked her hair softly and then gently raised her face, caressing its delicate contours. He kissed her on the forehead, holding her face in his hands, he kissed her lightly on each cheek, and then with all the passion that had been building from playful bantering and words that were spoken with hidden meanings, he found her lips. They were waiting to receive his kiss. A galaxy of stars exploded, illuminating the night and melting away the world, leaving only the two of them.

For a long time they stood just holding each other, lost in a space of time that would soon find its end. Anais stirred in Gathen's arms and reality rushed back like an unwelcome cold wind. Gathen whispered softly against her hair. "Will you marry me, Anais?"

Anais did not raise her head from his chest. Warm tears began to trickle down her cheeks, and she said in a muffled voice into his shirt, "Oh, Gathen, what have I done? What have I done?" A sob rose in her throat.

"I've so wanted to hear you say those words, and all along I have known that I had no right to want this—no right at all." She sobbed openly. Gathen held her away from him and looked at her, puzzled.

"Why? What's wrong, Anais?"

She gazed at him and shook her head slowly from side to side. "I wish with all my heart that there were just the two of us. I feel very much at peace with you, and I think that I love you very much, and I would have been so very proud to share your life." A sob caught in her throat. She tossed her dark hair back and said, "I'm engaged to be married. We've known each other a long time. Our families are friends and I suppose since the summer we met they have expected us to marry."

Anais could not see his eyes in the shadows, but she could feel them burning into hers. She turned from Gathen to stare out at the twinkling lights of the hill town.

"Wouldn't it be nice if we were seventeen? You do things when you are younger that you cannot do when you're older and have others to consider. That's the terrible thing about growing up, isn't it? Responsibility." Anais moved away with a sigh and said, "Happiness seems always to be flying away. One little flash and it's gone."

Gathen watched the back of her head as the light winds played gently with her hair.

"I love you, Gathen, even though the time we have known each other can be counted in hours." She gave a little sardonic laugh that was mixed with a whimper. "I'm going to have to be very strong because I want to run away with you."

"Why don't you?" he asked in earnest.

Anais went back to him. She put her hand to his face and brushed his hair back gently. His skin was damp and strands of hair clung to his forehead.

"How could I hurt Elliott so?" she replied, still stroking his hair away from his face. "Oh, my dearest, I have had so many of the good things that life has had to offer, and you can't have everything." She lowered her head. "I wish it had stopped somewhere else, not with you."

Anais smiled at him but he did not return her smile. He

was still young enough to challenge life's denials and he did not accept this rejection and he was angry. He looked away from her.

"Gathen," she appealed to him, "everything lies before you. I've never heard you play, but those who have say that you have a great talent, that of a genius, and you have worked so hard."

She leaned her head against his chest again, and he enfolded her in his arms, trying desperately to make her a part of him. "You will soon forget me, and tonight will just be a shadow in your memory." After a few moments he spoke.

"Let me be the judge of what memories I will hold. Anais, I would chuck every damn piano into the sea if it meant that I could have you."

She put her fingers to his lips to stem the pleas, but he removed her hand and continued. "I'm begging you, Anais, don't send me away. Without you nothing else matters."

"No! No! Gathen, you mustn't." There was a hint of anger in her voice. "I just can't walk away and hurt a person who has only been good and dear to me for many years." She looked at him beseechingly. They held each other's gaze and he slowly unfolded her from his arms and said, "If you say so, Anais."

The dark satiny night was spangled with lights from the hill town that winked in unison with the stars above, and the trees rustled rhythmically, filling the night air with the fragrant scent of pine, taunting the young lovers. Gathen heaved a sigh. This did not seem like the sort of night that would give birth to heartbreak.

Anais went through the French doors to her room. Gathen followed her to the door. "You can't dismiss love," he said. "You belong to me, Anais."

"I know," she replied and closed the door behind her.

CHAPTER 5

The sun was high in the sky as they drove back to Rome. Silence and loneliness filled the car. The bright sunlight only added to the desolation that engulfed them. They passed the Villa d'Este and the olive grove without comment. Along the way Gathen reached over and took Anais' hand and she curled her fingers around his.

"I'm playing at Adelaide's on Wednesday. Can you come?"

"I leave for New York Wednesday night. What time will you start?" she asked.

"Eight." He looked hopefully at Anais.

"I think so, but I won't be able to stay until the end," she replied.

"All right." He smiled at her. "I'm glad you will come, for whatever time."

The rest of the trip back to Rome was made in silence as they watched the pastoral landscape fade behind them.

Anais entered her apartment door and was met by a frantic Pina.

"*Signorina*, where have you been? We have been terrified for your safety. I expected you last evening." Pina stared at Anais with wide dark eyes that waited for an answer. Anais' head was splitting and she was not in a mood to hear of all the tragic thoughts that had gone through

Pina's mind, and she was sure, also Adelaide's. She sighed and merely said, "There was no need to worry. I'm quite all right. I'm sorry that you were upset." She patted Pina on the shoulder.

The telephone rang and Anais was much relieved for something else to do besides trying to soothe Pina's overwrought nerves. She picked up the receiver and said, "Hello."

"Anais, where have you been?" Adelaide said with a sigh of relief. "Never mind, as long as you're all right." Anais was glad that Adelaide was not insistent on an explanation.

"Elliott has been calling practically every hour on the hour. I told him that you were at my place in the country and the phone was disconnected. Well, I'm glad that you're back. Good-bye, dear." Adelaide broke the connection.

Whatever explanation Anais had to offer, clearly Adelaide did not want to hear it.

"Good-bye, Adelaide," Anais said frailly. She replaced the receiver on the hook and stood in deep solitude, back in the world of reality. Life seemed long and empty.

Wednesday arrived on a muted bustle. Luggage was piled high on the marble floor of the entrance hall, and the apartment had taken on a hollow emptiness and the disquieting sound of someone getting ready to go away for a long time.

Pina shuffled around the apartment, opening and closing bureau drawers and closet doors looking for some little thing that might have been missed, and just for something to do to hold back the constantly brimming tears. She was always overwhelmed by sadness when Anais returned to New York. Anais, too, had been on the brink of tears all morning and, at times, one or two would spill over and her nose became pink. Leaving Rome always made her sad, but it had never been like this.

In confusion and pain Anais sat before her dressing table putting finishing touches to her attire. She wore a raw-silk Chanel suit of beige with a creamy silk overblouse. She took a small gold brooch of delicate flowers studded with tiny diamonds and sapphires and placed it against her jacket. She gave it a critical look and placed it back in the jewel case. Pina's suggestion that she wear the brooch; it had always been a favorite of Pina's. Anais draped a double strand of pearls around her neck. That was better, she thought. She glanced at the brooch lying atop the other jewels and began to search through the dresser drawer for a piece of tissue paper. Anais found a piece and wrapped the brooch in it. She turned toward the door with a look of foreboding when she heard the muffled grunts and scuffling of the porters as they came in for the luggage. She heard the door shut and there was quiet again. Anais took her purse from the bed and gave the room a last look of tenderness.

"When will I see this room again?" she said softly. At that moment Pina came to the door and said, "Your taxi is here, signorina."

Anais sighed. "I'm coming." She and Pina embraced with affection. "I'll miss you, Pina."

And through much sniffling, Pina managed to say, "God bless you, signorina."

Anais placed the tissue paper in Pina's hand and said, "Wear it well, Pina." She hurried down the steps to the waiting lift. She did not look back but Pina heard her say, "Take care, Pina."

Pina watched the lift descend and then she opened the tissue paper and saw the delicate brooch glittering on the crumpled paper, and she whispered, "Oh, signorina." And the tears that had been held back all day flowed down her plump cheeks.

It was quarter to eight when Anais arrived at Adelaide's apartment. The hum of voices rose on the air as she entered the door. The air was charged with electricity as the elegantly dressed ladies and gentlemen milled around in great anticipation for the debut of the young pianist whom they had heard such marvelous things about.

Anais felt this excitement when she entered the room. Her simple suit stood out with grace as she made her way through the milling throng of floating silks and fluttering chiffons draped on all sizes and shapes of lovely women. She stopped and greeted some with a kiss, and some with a warm handshake. As she moved among the guests, Anais was careful not to move toward the group that Gathen was standing in, and she avoided looking in his direction for fear of catching his eye. And Gathen made no effort to come to her.

She found herself standing alone next to the dark glowing grand piano and started when Gathen spoke to her.

"However you feel about me, Anais, I don't believe that it is dislike." He smiled down at her. "So why try to avoid me?"

"I don't know, I suppose it's because I think that people

might know, if I looked at you," she stammered. "I don't know really." She looked down at her hands. Gathen looked around the room and said, "You see, no one is paying the slightest bit of attention to us." They stood looking at each other, and it was that moment that Anais knew where youth first takes its leave. "The eyes," she thought. She lowered her eyes, too pained to look at him any longer. She placed her hand over his long fingers that were resting on the piano and clasped them tightly and said, "I have no choice." She looked at him again. "I shall always think of you," she whispered.

"I will always remember," he said.

Wells Phipps strode toward them and stretched out his hands to Anais.

"Hello, Anais," he said, delighted to see her. He took both her hands in his and kissed her affectionately on each cheek.

"I'm sorry that you have to leave so soon, but we won't be far behind. We'll be in New York next month, and I think it will be Carnegie Hall. Not bad," he said with pride. Wells took Anais by the arm and led her to a chair next to Adelaide, who was already seated and beaming with delight in a lilac gown of peau de soie that billowed around her chair. She smiled at Anais.

Anais had not really been listening to Wells and had allowed herself to be led away from Gathen. Suddenly she realized that she had not said good-bye to him. But the room fell silent and she saw that Gathen had sat down to the piano. And Anais thought, "Not even to say good-bye. Oh, God! Oh, God!"

Adelaide leaned over and whispered to Anais, "I heard

him play this afternoon and oh-hh, Anais, he has magic." Adelaide was in exultation. Anais could see all of Adelaide's dreams bursting forth. Adelaide had sponsored a lot of artists but tonight she saw greatness.

Wells did not make an elaborate introduction, just "Ladies and gentlemen, Gathen Bentley." A long pause hung in the air and no one took a breath. Then the magic of Ludwig van Beethoven filled the room and Gathen Bentley's audience was intoxicated.

At nine forty-five, Anais turned quickly to Adelaide and kissed her on the cheek and said quietly, "Good-bye, darling, see you in New York." She hurried through the heavy carved doors without looking back and was unaware that for a moment Adelaide forgot the concert and watched her through the doors with a puzzled expression on her face. In all the years of their coming to and leaving Rome, she had never seen Anais near tears.

Anais thought that Gathen had not known when she left, but he had known the moment she whispered good-bye to Adelaide.

Anais walked out into the dark night, where the air now held a definite hint of fall. She stepped into the waiting taxi and leaned her head into the corner of the car, and the tears that could no longer be restrained poured down her cheeks and gave way to heartbreaking sobs. The taxi driver was prudent: he only looked in the rearview mirror once.

CHAPTER 6

When the concert came to a close, the applause and the shouts of "Bravo!" were deafening. Gathen bowed his thanks of their appreciation and their acceptance of his talent. After ten minutes of this, the guests surged around him, each personally wanting to wish him well.

A regaling party followed, but Gathen only stayed a short while, and Adelaide was not offended when he left quietly.

The following day Wells was greeted by a disheveled young man with red-rimmed glassy eyes and hair that was mussed and hung limply. Wells looked at Gathen curiously and said, "Man, you look terrible."

Gathen replied, "If it means anything, I feel as bad as I look."

He ran shaking fingers through his tangled hair. Wells mashed a cigarette out in a nearby ashtray. He looked at Gathen thoughtfully, then thrust his hands deep into his trouser pockets and said, "You don't have to say anything if you don't want to, Gathen, but I am a little concerned to see my meal ticket with hands that he can't hold steady."

Wells paused for a moment. "It's Anais, isn't it?" He waited for a moment, then said, "You don't have to answer; your silence tells me that it is."

Gathen turned away to look miserably out of the window.

Wells continued, "I had a feeling that I had interrupted something when I barged in at Adelaide's last night. I didn't know how to turn things around after I had walked into it without making things even more awkward. Sorry, Gathen."

Gathen continued to look out of the window, saying nothing.

Wells said, "From the look on Anais' face, I would gather that she feels the same way about you." He shrugged his shoulders. "And due to circumstances . . . you've both decided to call your feelings for each other off. Man, if that were only possible." He snapped his fingers and said, "Just like that, 'I don't love you and you don't love me.' Simple. Why doesn't it work that way? Then no one is hurt." Wells seemed to be talking more to himself than to Gathen, who still made no attempt to answer him.

Wells ignored Gathen's silence and continued. "If it's any consolation to you, Gathen, others have fallen in love with Anais, some passionately, and she has never shown the least bit of interest in any of them. But last night she was hurting. This time the love was returned, and that's something in itself, isn't it?" Wells looked for some words that would bring a little comfort to his friend.

Wells gave a smirk of a laugh and said, "I even toyed with the idea of falling in love with her myself. Besides her beauty, she is a remarkably nice woman."

With a great deal of effort Gathen managed to ask, "What sort of guy is this fiancé of hers?"

"Elliott." Wells turned the corners of his mouth down. "Pleasant enough, I suppose, eager-beaver type. He's from the same money and background as Anais. They more or less grew up together; families are friends. That sort of thing."

Gathen listened with veiled emotions as Wells's voice droned on and on. "You won't see much of him at Adelaide's soirees. He's usually off somewhere making deals. I don't know much else about him except that they say he worships Anais, but . . ." Wells left the rest of his thoughts hanging in the air. He saw no reason to comment any further on Elliott. He did not really like the man, and this had no bearings on his relationship with Anais. Regardless of what he thought.

Wells put his hand on the doorknob to leave. He turned once again to Gathen and said, "I'm truly sorry. I wish it could have been different. You're two nice people." Wells was thoughtful for a moment. "In time you will learn to live with it."

Wells was still thoughtful, then he said, "It's something in itself that she loved you, you know."

Gathen finally spoke. "I can't tell you how much I love her."

"You don't have to."

Gathen smiled at him and said, "That bad."

Wells said, "That bad." And they grinned at each other. "See you later, pal." Wells closed the door behind himself.

Gathen was left in a room that buzzed with silence and throbbed with loneliness. He pressed his fingers over his eyes to relieve some of the pressure of his aching head. Behind closed eyes he thought of Anais. He remembered her standing at the piano and telling him that she would always think of him; he tried to picture her at that moment and what she might be doing now. Gathen drew in a deep breath and thought that if he did not move right now he would never come to terms with this. So, with a great deal of effort, he heaved himself up and hurried to the bathroom. He turned the shower on and stripped off his clothes in seconds and stepped into the rushing water. He let the cool waters of the Eternal City wash over his weary body, washing away the dullness that grief had laden it with. The fine spiny spray brought life back to his body.

Gathen dressed in minutes and ran down the stone steps onto the street, where white sunlight dazzled the cobblestones under a clear blue sky.

There was no white sunlight spreading its rays of warmth to greet Anais, as the sun in Rome had greeted Gathen, but a cool gray oppressive day heavy with rain that hovered in the air but would not fall. Anais went quickly through customs and was met by her father's chauffeur, who had been waiting patiently for her plane to land; it was an hour late because of the weather. He touched the visor of his cap to her and said, "Hope your trip wasn't too bad, Miss LaPrell."

"Not too bad, Timothy. Just a little long." Anais smiled resignedly. "I'll go to my parents' apartment first," she said, handing her overnight case to Timothy.

"Yes, ma'am. I think they'll be very glad to see you."

They arrived at Anais' parents' Park Avenue apartment without any delays in traffic. Timothy let Anais out, giving her only the box that contained her mother's dress, which she juggled at the door as she waited for someone to answer her ring.

"Miss LaPrell. How nice to see you," the maid said, taking the box from Anais. "Your mother is in the sitting room."

"Thank you, Rose. I'll go straight in." Anais inquired about Rose's health and her family as Rose led her to her mother.

The woman who sat waiting in the splendid sitting room would never have been able to deny being the mother of the young woman who entered the room and said "Mother" with a deep joy. The woman rose from some papers that she had been going over when she heard her daughter's voice. Her shimmering white hair was cut shorter than Anais' but still in the same style, parted in the center with feathered wings cut at the temples. Her eyes were the same magnificent topaz as Anais'. They were the eyes of the Jardine family of Bethel, Virginia, and were passed on through the genes from generation to generation, and upon meeting strangers in town, members of the family would often be greeted with "You must be one of the Jardines."

Anais and her mother embraced warmly and her mother said, "Darling, I'm so glad you're home. How was the flight?" She fussed over Anais like any mother hen with just one chick. She studied Anais for a split second without making Anais aware of it, and her eyes narrowed quickly. She had the maid bring in some coffee and over her coffee cup she finally said what was on her mind. "Anais, I don't like the way you look. What's wrong?"

Anais shook her hair back and said jokingly, "Why,

Mother, I always thought you were pleased with the way I look. Everyone says I'm the spit and image of you." Anais spoke with an exaggerated southern accent.

"Oh, don't be silly, Anais, you know very well what I mean. There are dark shadows under your eyes."

Anais became serious and said, "It's just the time change, and I'm tired."

Her mother, unconvinced by Anais' explanation, dropped the subject and said, "Timothy can take you home as soon as your father and Andy get here."

Anais left her chair and exclaimed, "Oh, I brought your dress. Angelina outdid herself with this one." Anais brought the box to her mother and put it on the table. Together they opened the box.

"Oh, it is beautiful," her mother exclaimed, holding the dress against her still-slim body.

"It goes beautifully with your hair, Mother," Anais said, standing back in admiration of her sublime mother.

As they stood admiring the dress, the door suddenly opened with a rush of wind and a small boy entered the room on its wake crying, "Hi, Aunt Anais." He ran to his aunt's outstretched arms. Anais rubbed the boy's knees and said, "Oooh-hh, you have cold knees." The six-year-old boy, whose dark hair hung over his Jardine golden eyes in bangs, gave his aunt another big hug as she tried to warm his cold knees with her hands. She looked on the small boy with the love of a mother.

The child's mother had been Anais' only sister, whom Anais had loved dearly; they had shared so much of their young lives together.

Anais' eyes fixed on the boy as her thoughts traveled back to one tragic New Year's Eve night when Julia had wanted to show off her expertise as a balloonist and had invited family and friends down to the meadows to watch as she and some of her friends cast off in her beautiful brightly colored prized balloon, with lovely, joyous, and reckless Julia, who loved every moment of life at the helm.

The balloon began its ascent. Releasing its mooring ropes, it rose gracefully from the ground with its basket of tittering passengers swaying gaily in the night breeze. Suddenly an erratic wind caused the balloon to veer off its course across the meadows and drift toward the nearby highway, and without warning the dark winter's night exploded in blinding yellow flames as the balloon touched a high-tension wire, silhouetting against its light a convulsed crowd of people thrown into a nightmare. Passing motorists jumped from their cars and tried to help, but it was no use. When they pulled her sister and friends from the blackened basket, it was too late. At that moment, Anais was still listening to the screams.

"Aunt Anais?" She heard a small voice calling her back from that tragic night. She saw her nephew regarding her with a puzzled look on his face. Anais quickly recovered and said, "I was just thinking, darling, that you will soon be going to school and we're going to have to go shopping for school clothes and pads and pencils for such a big boy. Oh, my," she said out loud, and thought to herself, "Oh, how I wish your mother could see you."

She turned and looked at her mother, who was also watching her grandson. Her mother now seemed on the road to living with the terrible tragedy of losing a child. "Only to live with," she thought, "never to recover, and it always seems that it happened just yesterday."

A big man, with hair that was almost white, entered the

room. Anais stood up to greet him. He put both of his big hands on her shoulders and bent to kiss her on the cheek; just one cheek, not the chic European way of two light pecks on each cheek, and if he'd traveled to Europe every day of the year he would still be just what he was born, a Texan.

"Hello, Daddy," Anais said, stretching up to reach his cheek as he bent to kiss her.

"Good to have you home, honey," he said, putting his arm around her waist.

Anais leaned her head against his shoulder and said, "It's good to be home." But as she spoke those words, her mother scrutinized her for a moment and she thought that her daughter's words did not ring true, and she said to her husband, "Anais is very tired. Now that you and Andy are here, Timothy can take her home. Andy, you can go to the door with your aunt and then you, Grandpa, and Grandma will have lunch."

She watched her six-year-old grandson with loving eyes as he pulled up a gray knee sock.

"Okay," he said without ceremony as he concentrated on his sock. "Grandpa and I have something to do later on." The boy suddenly jumped up and leaped into the arms of his grandfather, who caught him with a big hug.

Anais' mother pressed a button beside the fireplace, which was burning brightly on its first day of the season. Rose entered the room on the summons of the bell.

"Mrs. LaPrell," she answered the call as she stood in the doorway.

"Rose, will you tell Timothy that Miss LaPrell is ready to go home?"

After Anais and Andy left the room her mother remained by the fireplace with a look of concern clouding her eyes.

"I really think that Arthur should spend more time with Andy," she said. "He is certainly not being a responsible father."

"Well, honey, Arthur had some important business down in Paraguay, and he's not a nine-to-five man," her husband said soothingly.

"Neither were you, and you never neglected your duties as a father," she said, refusing to excuse Arthur's continuous absence.

"But you must remember, my dear, that my father left me an enormous fortune. I didn't have to try as hard as Arthur, and your father didn't do badly by you either." He laughed at his wife's inability to understand the businessman's mind.

"What you are saying is that business matters are more important than taking the time to see that your son has grown an inch." She hugged her shoulders and sat down in a comfortable chair before the fire.

Her husband could always tell the moment that their lost daughter came across his wife's mind, and he said tenderly, "Andy knows that he is greatly loved." He stood beside her and gently put his hand on her shoulder, and she caressed it and smiled up at him.

"I know, and if there was such a thing as too much love, the scales would certainly tip in that direction." She looked thoughtful again. "I'm a little worried about Anais. She didn't seem quite right to me."

"Well, she's gone home to Tillie, and heaven knows,

dear, Tillie thinks that she is the only thing that Anais ever needed."

The sky was beginning to clear a bit over the East River, but the day remained raw and damp. When Anais arrived at her house on Sutton Place, she was glad to be home. She could relax, especially since Elliott had not met her at the airport. Anais unlocked the door onto a marble black-and-white diamond-patterned foyer that contained only a large ornately carved Italian Renaissance cabinet and a gold altar light with a red glass candle holder hung from the ceiling.

A plump woman with graying wiry hair that made a halo around her pink smooth face came across the marble floor from the kitchen area. She wore a gray uniform with a thin white apron. She held out her ample arms and took Anais to her breast.

"Anais," she said with love. It would always be "Anais." Tillie had been there when Anais was born and she was there through everything that concerned Anais. And again Anais was fussed over and carefully scrutinized.

"All this traveling around from country to country. I'll never understand. People should stay at home where they belong," she fussed. That was Tillie's way of saying that Anais did not look right to her, without actually saying the words.

Anais put her arm around Tillie and said, "Fuss, fuss. Tillie, you should come to Italy with us."

"I don't need to see nothing outside this country, thank you."

"You're just an old chauvinist." Anais laughed.

"Why don't you go upstairs and rest? I'll help Timothy with your bags," Tillie said.

"I think I'll do just that." She made a sad attempt at being cheerful. Once in her room Anais lost herself in the whirlpool of confusion that had been threatening to engulf her all day, and she lay across her bed and wept. When her sobbing subsided, Anais ran a bath filled with perfumed bubbles of white foam. She lay deep in the pleasing water and tried to soak away the ache in her heart. She clasped a hand that was encrusted with a rainbow of bubbles to her hair and said aloud, "I should not be this unhappy. I'm going to marry a very fine man that I have known most of my life, whom I love and who loves me." And she wiped away the tears with the soft bath sponge. "What is wrong with me?"

Anais slept on Roman time and awakened somewhere near four o'clock in the morning. The moon still shone, marking a pale silver path across the dark turbulent waters of the East River. She lay in bed and watched a cloud float across the face of the moon hiding its beams from the river, leaving it without a glow. She arose from her bed and went to the bay window and sat on the seat beneath it. She pulled her warm dressing gown around her against the chill of the morning and watched an unblemished dawn give birth to a new day, and she wondered how she could ever face it.

At 10 A.M. Anais went downstairs. She could not put off facing Tillie another moment or she was sure Tillie would come up to her room.

"Good morning," Anais said with the same cheerful voice that she had affected yesterday. "Was it only two days ago that I said good-bye to Gathen? It seems like a million years ago," she thought as she poured a cup of coffee. She was so lost in her thoughts that she did not hear Tillie speak to her. She turned to see Tillie looking at her with a puzzled expression on her kind face.

"I said Mr. Barclay called." Tillie always called Elliott Mr. Barclay. "I told him that you were asleep. He said he'd call back."

"Oh" was the only word that Anais could think of.

"You look better today." Tillie still held Anais under scrutiny. "But still a little pale. Oh, and Timothy's bringing Andy over. He wants to go to the zoo."

"All right. We can do some shopping too"—Anais smiled with real pleasure—"and get him ready for his big debut." Anais' thoughts swallowed her up again. "So this is how it is, as if nothing has changed and everyday life goes on as if there had never been that time of love."

Three weeks passed and Adelaide arrived back in New York and the new season was about to begin. New plays were opening on Broadway and concerts were starting at Carnegie Hall. Adelaide called in a prismatic flurry. Gathen was going to make his debut at Carnegie Hall on the twelfth of October. Anais' heart pounded furiously in her chest.

"You are coming? Let me get tickets with my party for you and Elliott." Anais' mind was racing, trying to think of an excuse not to go, and certainly not with Elliott.

"Let me see, Adelaide. Elliott is out of town, and I don't

know what his plans will be. But don't put me down just yet," she said.

"Well, all right, dear, but do try to come. There will be a big party afterward, and his parents will be here from South Carolina. I'll speak to you later. Good-bye, dear." And Adelaide was gone, but she had left Anais with a throbbing headache.

The following days before the concert were hectic ones for Adelaide. The sale of the tickets and preparation for the party after the concert occupied her every thought, which left her little time for Anais. This was a blessing to Anais, who only wanted to be alone with her own thoughts. Elliott telephoned her every day, since his business was keeping him in Montreal. He apologized, but he would be home as soon as he possibly could. So Anais bought one ticket in the balcony. The seat was not bad, but far from the dress circle where Adelaide and her friends would be seated.

CHAPTER 7

The night of the concert found the city blanketed under a drizzly October sky. The flaming leaves of autumn clung to the dark branches of the trees spattered with shiny drops of rain. Anais arrived unobtrusively at Carnegie Hall in a taxi, wearing a plain black broadtail coat and a wide floppy black hat that covered most of her lovely face.

The crowd milled about in the lobby waiting to go in. Anais stepped in among them and made her way up the steps to the balcony. Wells, who was roaming about the lobby, noticed the attractive woman ascending the stairs and suddenly raised his hand to signal her as he recognized the woman to be Anais. But she hurried up the steps and Wells was left holding his arm in the air. Later, backstage, he mentioned to Adelaide that he had seen Anais.

"How odd" was Adelaide's only comment. Gathen was silent but he had overheard Wells tell Adelaide that Anais was there.

The usher showed Anais to her seat, as the house began to fill with the excitement of restrained hubbub. Then a sudden hush fell over the audience as the conductor came out onto the stage, then a burst of applause sounded throughout the perfect acoustical walls. The conductor bowed low and pointed his baton in the direction of the wings, where a tall handsome young man in white tie and tails appeared. He walked to the piano through thundering applause and bowed his head to the audience. He looked up in the direction of the balcony: even though he could not see anyone through the veil of lights, he knew that Anais was there and he bowed to her. Her eyes filled with tears.

The beautiful strains of a Brahms piano concerto flowed through the hall from the fingers of Gathen. Anais watched his every movement and, though the music was Brahms and the instrument was the piano, Anais could only see a salmon-pink sky and hear the soft melodious strings of a guitar that had never been played properly until that day. Anais closed her eyes and listened to "Ramona."

The concert came to an end to thunderous applause. But Gathen did not return for a curtain call. Instead he rushed from the hall out into the now steady rain to see if he could catch Anais. As he reached the front of the hall, she was already getting into a waiting taxi. Gathen stood for a few minutes in the gutter, where the rushing water that was colored by the lights from the neon signs carried brown autumn leaves in its stream, dampening his feet. He took no notice. His only thoughts were on the taxicab that maneuvered its way around the line of waiting limousines and headed toward Fifth Avenue. A curious crowd was beginning to gather when he turned with a rain-sprinkled face and went back to the hall.

With Gathen's rush from the hall, Adelaide commented to Wells, "This is all very odd."

"Beats me," Wells replied innocently.

"I'm not certain I believe that," Adelaide said. But Wells

was saved any further embellishment of his untruth by the reappearance of a somewhat soggy Gathen, who, for appearance' sake, seemed to recover his sense of well-being immediately upon seeing the photographers. He smiled with the self-assurance of a man who had made his mark.

"Ah! There you are, darling." Adelaide went to Gathen with outstretched arms, and the cameras began to click. There were photographs taken of Gathen with his parents and Adelaide, with Wells, and one in which Gathen's mother insisted upon having a starry-eyed, dewy-skinned girl with honey-colored hair named Barbara Ann in the picture with them. The girl gazed up at Gathen with all the adoration of a high school sweetheart, and that is exactly what the newspapers called her the next day in their report.

Anais went through all the morning papers and clipped out the reviews on Gathen. They were all glowing reports, but her heart faltered at the sight of the girl. She stacked all the papers together and placed the clippings in a scrapbook. Anais went to the window and gazed at the slate-colored waters of the turbulent East River. She felt dull and excluded. A sharp pang of jealousy and the uselessness of it all overwhelmed her.

The gray smoke from the three smokestacks of Con Edison climbed into the dark clouds that were pouring rain over the city. Anais traced with her fingers silver rivulets of raindrops as they slithered down the windowpane. Slowly, burning tears began to drop from her eyes, and in a surge of frustration she leaned her head against the cold windowpane and pounded the glass with her fist.

"Oo-hh, lambie! Lambie!" Tillie cried from behind

Anais. "What's the matter? What's the matter?" She took Anais away from the window and sat her down on the bed; she sat down beside her and held Anais' head against her breast. Tillie smoothed Anais' hair back from her face and cooed to her.

"There, there, now. Hush, hush, my little lamb. Hush."

After a few moments of heartbreaking sobbing, Anais regained her composure. She sat dabbing her eyes with her handkerchief. Tillie looked at her sternly but not without sympathy and asked, "What on earth is the matter, Anais?"

Anais choked on a sob and replied, "Oh, I can't tell you, Tillie, I can't tell you." And she began to weep again.

In exasperation, Tillie said, "Well, I've never heard that before. What in the name of heaven is wrong in this family anyway? Everyone seems to have the heebie-jeebies around here."

Anais did not answer Tillie; she continued to look down at her crumpled handkerchief. She finally spoke through hiccups.

"I think I'll go up to the house in Connecticut for a few days."

Tillie spoke to Anais angrily. "Do you know what I think? I think you people have too many houses. If something goes wrong, you pick up and run to another house. But you forget that you take yourself with you. And until you resolve it here and here"—Tillie pointed to her head and to her heart—"everything remains the same, no matter where you are."

"Then do you mind if I go for a walk?" Anais asked childishly.

"Go to Connecticut. And if you go for a walk put some rubbers on."

That was the end of what Tillie had to say and she went back to the kitchen, but she knew that the newspaper clippings had something to do with Anais' tears.

Anais did not wish to raise Tillie's ire again, so she went to the hall closet to get a raincoat and boots. She could not find her boots in the closet. She had not worn them for a while and could not imagine where they might be. Anais was just getting ready to call to Tillie when she heard the doorbell. She started to answer the door but Tillie was already there, and she was just closing it again when Anais appeared on the stairs. She saw Tillie holding a square white box that was tied with a lavender ribbon.

"What is it, Tillie?" Anais looked at the box with curiosity.

"Must be flowers, but there's no florist's name on the box. It's for you," Tillie said, handing the box to Anais, and watched her untie the ribbon. Tillie's curiosity was as awakened now as Anais'. Anais gently pushed the tissue paper surrounding the gift. At first no words would come. She could only smile with the greatest of joy as she carefully lifted the blossom from its bed of tissue paper.

"Oh! Isn't it beautiful, Tillie?" Anais' golden eyes filled with love.

"Who's it from?" Tillie asked.

"There's no card," Anais answered, still looking at the flower.

"Where on earth would anyone get a magnolia this time of year?" Tillie asked, with more curiosity than joy, and with the look on Anais' face, Tillie did not have to say, "But you know who it's from," as she studied Anais' face.

"I'll get something to put it in," Tillie offered.

"No, thank you, Tillie, I'll take it to my room. I have a vase there."

Anais walked up the stairs as if in a dream, tenderly examining every little detail of the beautiful white fragrant flower.

Tillie watched Anais as she walked up the stairs and shook her head sadly and said to herself, "I never did like that Barclay. Him and his highfalutin' airs. Humph." Tillie's final thought for Elliott Barclay was, "It's not too late to change your mind."

In a few days the lovely white waxy petals opened and turned brown. The petals drooped sadly around the crystal vase, its beauty gone. Anais took the limp flower and wrapped it in a piece of plastic; she placed it in a scrapbook that she had just for Gathen. She then put it far back on a shelf in her closet. Elliott called to say that he had just arrived and was in his office.

When the phone rang, Anais was absorbed with her plans for the day, which mainly concerned her family. She would take Andy shopping for school clothes, then they would have lunch at the zoo in Central Park, and Andy would have one of his special treats, riding downtown to Wall Street with Timothy to pick up his grandfather from his office.

The phone interrupted Anais' thoughts. She reached for the unwelcome intrusion and lifted the receiver, and Elliott's voice boomed through the wires.

"Hello, darling!"

"Hello, Elliott." Anais smiled faintly, trying to bring some measure of cheer to her voice.

"Look, darling," Elliott continued with exuberance, "I've got a meeting in about ten minutes. Let's say dinner at eight-thirty at Aurore's. I'll pick you up at eight." The phone buzzed in her ear. She regarded the receiver in her hand before replacing it in its cradle. "Oh, Elliott." He had disconnected without allowing her to say anything at all.

After spending the morning shopping for Andy's approaching schooldays, and having an unmentionable lunch at the zoo, Anais and Andy headed home to his grandmother, where Andy promptly showed off his new school supplies. He had just finished when Timothy rang up on the house phone to ask if he was ready to go downtown to meet his grandfather.

The room fell silent with Andy's departure. Anais sat down on the sofa and stretched her long legs out in front of her and said, "Your grandson has a lot of energy." Her mother nodded her head. "Well do I know that," she said smiling.

Anais' eyes became sad and she sighed. "I wish Julia could see him now."

Her mother's eyes moistened and she said, "I know, darling."

Anais stared straight ahead, her eyes narrowed as they tried to look back into the past.

"Do you know, Mother, I've had the strangest feeling that something was troubling Julia before"—Anais stammered over the word that she still found difficult to say—

"before she died. I don't know, she seemed preoccupied and subdued. And I have never understood why she waived her rights to any inheritance from Daddy in her will."

Her mother looked worried and said, "I suppose we'll never know now."

Anais sighed and left the sofa. "I suppose not." She gathered her belongings and prepared to leave.

"I'm having dinner with Elliott tonight." Anais wanted to change the subject; she did not want to think that Julia had felt the coming of death.

Her mother had been ready to end the conversation also, and she asked, "Where are you and Elliott having dinner?"

"At Aurore's," Anais replied.

"Trust Elliott to go to the showiest place in town." She walked with Anais to the door.

"I think I shall now walk home," she said, smiling, "and see if I can walk down the zoo's lunch."

Darkness had already fallen, though the hour was still early, as Anais made her way unhurriedly across a tree-lined East Sixty-fifth Street. Just ahead of her a black limousine pulled up to the curb, the driver got out to open the door, but the passengers in the back seat were alighting from the car before he could get around to their side.

Two men looked familiar to Anais, as their shadowy figures moved away from the car toward one of the town houses. She reached the men just as they started up the steps and recognition was simultaneous.

"Anais." The two men spoke at once.

"Why, Elliott and Arthur!" Surprise was in Anais' voice. "Arthur, I thought you were still in Paraguay."

Both men kissed her.

"Darling, this is Mr. Eric von Stressmann, and Senator Bain."

"Charmed, Miss LaPrell," von Stressmann said with a slight click of his heels as he touched her fingers to his lips. He held both her hands in his and patted them gently. He smiled down at her with hooded eyes that slanted downward and said to Elliott, "Such a lovely young lady. I hope that you will not keep her just to yourself." He patted Anais' hand again. "Elliott tells me that you have just returned from Rome. We must talk sometime of Rome."

Anais found this fatherly gentleman utterly charming and was about to extend an invitation when another figure came up behind her. In the darkness Anais did not recognize the man, but when Elliott spoke his name, Anais knew immediately who the man was. Kincade Hogg, the ultraright-wing Texas oilman who, Anais was certain, had he lived during the Revolutionary War would have been a Tory. Anais said good-bye, with Elliott asking if she thought it safe to walk home alone, and reminding her that he would pick her up at eight. In the tense air she heard Elliott say in an agitated tone, "Don't worry about it."

The rest of Anais' walk home was spent in a confusion of thoughts. She had not realized that Arthur and Elliott had any business associations, and she could not understand their acquaintance with the archconservative senator or Kincade Hogg. The senator's quiet eyes and white hair gave him a boyish look even though he was well into his fifties. His boyish innocence gave belief to his staunch support of morality and whatever was for the good of the country, and he never failed to remind his constituents that he, the good senator, was from a humble background. The senator never thought it necessary to remind his constituents that he was a self-made millionaire on a congressional salary, and that what was good for the senator was good for the country, and his loyal constituents rewarded him each election year by voting him back into the Senate.

When Elliott arrived at eight he had the taxi wait while he called for Anais, who was dressed and ready. They were whisked off to the elegant Aurore's.

The waiter pulled the table aside and Anais slipped into the apple-green plush velvet upholstered seat. As Elliott settled himself in the chair opposite her, Anais regarded him with narrowed eyes. His dark pinstripe suit with vest and perfectly knotted tie was impeccable, and his hair was too tightly brushed and a bit too shiny. With the long cool gaze that she had fixed on him, Anais realized that she would not marry Elliott.

Elliott mistakenly took the gaze as one of affection; he reached across the table and took both Anais' hands into his. Under the pretense of straightening the silver, Anais removed her hands from his clasp.

CHAPTER 8

The rays of the sun were long and slanting and the vivid red and gold of the autumn leaves had disappeared from the trees, leaving stark-naked branches against a pale sky. The onset of winter found Anais in better spirits. Gathen was on a concert tour and she kept up with it as best she could. When she knew the city he was playing in, she would go down to Times Square and get the out-of-town newspaper and clip the reviews. The raw pain of missing Gathen was now just a dull ache. She saw Adelaide often, and she had resumed her social life. She often went to pick Andy up after school. He felt very grown up and complained that he could go home alone.

"That," Anais drove home to him, "will be quite some time to come." So he settled down and enjoyed his aunt's coming for him after school.

Elliott still spent most of the time away on business trips. In the business world this is considered normal. Most women soon adjust to this and learn to live on their own, and some even manage to enjoy the absence of the men. And with a twinge of guilt feelings, Anais was not unhappy that Elliott was not about that often.

With the holidays approaching, Elliott's thoughts, like those of most businessmen, would soon turn toward home.

Anais announced to Tillie, one chilly November morning, that she was going up to the house in Connecticut. "But, Tillie, it's to get the house ready for Thanksgiving. I want to help Helga and Karl to get the Christmas decorations down from the attic before Thanksgiving. We never have enough time those few days we're up there, and before you know it, it's Christmas," she said cheerfully.

The bare branches of the trees hummed softly in the wind as dark and ominous clouds brooded overhead. Anais stepped from the car into the brisk air; her tweed jacket and woolen skirt were not quite enough against the November chill and she hurried into the large white Colonial house that sat among winter trees on a circular drive hidden from the main road by acres of land. The dark-green shutters at the windows looked bright on such a bleak day. When Anais entered the large center hall, Helga, the housekeeper, greeted her warmly in her still-heavy German accent. Helga and her husband, Karl, were caretakers, who resided in a charming cottage a short distance from the main house, and usually lived undisturbed by the owners except for holidays and occasional times when city noise could no longer be tolerated.

The dark wide-board floors were highly polished and were scattered with rare antique oriental rugs. Fine furniture of the American past filled the house, and beautiful fringed curtains of heavy silk hung at the windows. A cheerful fire burned in the white wood-paneled fireplace with the smell of burning logs, and the quiet coziness of the house made Anais glad that she had come.

"You will have some lunch now?" Helga asked as Anais went to warm her hands at the fire.

"Yes. I think I will have it in here," Anais answered.

drapes back. There in the undergrowth were distinct automobile tracks. Broken branches hung from the bushes where the car had squeezed into the thicket. Anais called Karl to the window.

"Look, Karl, there has been someone here!" she said with excitement pitching her voice. Karl looked at the wheel marks with concern spreading in his pale-blue eyes. "I'd better call the police," he said.

The police arrived in about fifteen minutes. They walked around the grounds with Karl and Anais and searched the cottage and ascertained that nothing had been taken. One of the policemen said, "We try to patrol the place as often as we can, but sometimes they come in by the back road around the lake. The youngsters sort of use the place as a lovers' lane. We'll try to step up the patrol."

"Well, nice seeing you, Miss LaPrell." They touched the tips of their caps and got back into the patrol car. Anais and Karl watched the car back out and pull away. Somehow Anais' instinct ran contrary to that of the police, and she saw more to the intrusion than just young lovers looking for a place to be alone.

Anais stayed one more night. She went through the Christmas decorations with love and tenderness. Some of the ornaments dated back to before she and Julia were born. Anais held a shiny red ball up and the lamp played with the lights in it, and for a few moments through the little pinpoint of light Anais was ferried back through the passage of memory to the magic of childhood at Christmastime, where there were only small hurts that could be cured by a kiss from Mommy and Daddy.

Anais heard herself giggle as her father held her up so

"Good. I will bring," Helga said, leaving the room. Anais gazed long into the yellow crackling flames and her mind wandered back to the house in the country in Italy.

Helga soon returned with a tray and placed it on the mahogany table in front of the fire. Helga's return drew Anais back from her thoughts with a start. She looked up quickly, as if Helga might have been able to read her mind.

"Oh! Helga, you startled me." Anais laughed, somewhat disoriented by her silliness. She sat down on the sofa in front of the tray. Helga busily put things in place and chatted away while she did so.

"When Mr. Carlyle and Mr. Barclay were here last week with some gentlemen, they did not want me to serve them, just cook and clean up the dishes. Didn't seem right having guests and making them do for themselves." Helga shook her head silently as if trying to bring something that was in the back of her mind to the forefront, but it kept eluding her. Anais could only stare at Helga in astonishment. Helga left the room with a puzzled look on her round face. Anais was even more puzzled, since Arthur was supposed to have been in Paraguay and Elliott in Montreal.

Anais sat on the side of her canopied bed looking as if she belonged in a bygone year, her smoky hair spread about the shoulders of the poet-sleeved white nightgown that had a blue silk ribbon running through the pleated yoke and a small border of lace on the collar.

The day had gone well as far as getting the Christmas decorations in order was concerned, but the puzzle of Elliott and Arthur was preying on her mind and refused to be dismissed by reasoning that Arthur certainly had access to the house—after all he had spent years here off and on with Julia. "But why not say so?" Her thoughts spoke out loud. He certainly had the opportunity and he had made no effort to see Andy.

Anais was still mulling these disturbing things in her mind when the wind began to rise and the trees lashed back and forth in a fury as the heavy clouds pelted the earth with huge drops of rain. Anais went quickly to pull the window down, when through the dark and swaying trees she caught a glimpse of light coming from the old cottage that was once used as a guesthouse; but guests now always stayed in the main house, unless someone wanted a complete retreat when they came to visit. The yellow light glowed briefly through the trees and went out.

Anais pressed her head against the post of the bed as she sat on the edge. She was, to say the least, a little frightened. She started to pick up the phone and call Karl, but decided against it. She looked at the clock: it was late and Karl would go to investigate and might get hurt. Anais went back to the window and peered out. There was only darkness. She left the window and got into bed.

She thought, "Could I have imagined the light? No, I did not," she concluded.

At eight o'clock the next morning, Anais went down to the kitchen, where she knew she would find Helga.

"Helga," Anais began without salutation, "is there anyone down at the guest cottage?"

"Why, no, Miss LaPrell. There's no one here but Karl and me. Why do you ask?" Helga asked, just as puzzled as Anais.

"I think I saw a light on down there last night," Anais said.

"The electricity is off. Been off a long time," Helga answered.

"I think I'll go down and have a look. Perhaps my imagination ran away with the storm." She smiled at Helga.

"Wait, I will call Karl. You can never tell—a vagrant might have wandered in out of the rain."

Anais waited at the back door for Karl, who came in heavy work boots and carrying a big stick.

Anais trekked over the soggy ground with the mud sometimes nearly covering the top of her shoes, which prompted Karl to say, "You should have worn some other shoes. I'll clean those when we get back." At that moment Karl's foot slipped into a deep mudhole and he swore discreetly under his breath as Anais helped him to extricate his foot.

Although the cottage was well kept it looked sad and abandoned. "We must do something about this cottage. It shouldn't just sit like this. Perhaps one of Adelaide's protégés could use it. It's rather a pretty little house," she said.

Karl took a key ring that held a jumble of keys and unlocked the door. It opened onto a charming sitting room that held a large porcelain stove that sat between two heavily curtained windows. Anais and Karl walked around the room carefully. Karl opened the door to the bedroom, where neatly made twin rosewood beds took up most of the room. Anais examined the bureau drawers and found nothing there. She went to the window and pulled the that she could reach a branch to hang the shimmering red ball. Julia stood on the floor giggling through her fingers that were clasped tightly over her mouth for fear that Anais would drop the ornament. From the floor, where she sat surrounded by Christmas decorations, Anais could smell the fragrance of the fir tree and hear the bells of Christmas. She leaned back against the foot of the bed and dreamed of the past. It took a few moments before she realized that the Christmas bells was the telephone ringing. She hurried up to the phone and was surprised to hear Elliott's lighthearted voice say, "Darling, I didn't know you were going to the country."

When Anais arrived back at the house in New York, Tillie met her at the door and told her, "Your father wants you to call him right away. He said it's important." Tillie was noncommittal as she went back to what she had been doing before Anais came in.

"Is he downtown or at home?" Anais called to Tillie's disappearing back.

"Downtown," Tillie called back as she went through the door.

Anais went into the library and telephoned her father. She first reached his secretary, who put her through to her father immediately.

"Daddy, is there anything wrong?" she asked anxiously.

"Hello, honey. It's not serious. But do you remember the bonds your uncle gave Julia for a wedding present?"

"Yes," she replied still puzzled.

"Did Julia give them to you?" her father asked, and without waiting for an answer he continued: "E.B. says that he heard that they were floating on the market." He paused. "I was just wondering if you needed money."

"Why, no. I don't know anything about it. Is Uncle E.B. sure?"

E.B. was Anais' father's brother, and his Christian name was abbreviated to his initials because he could not stand his first name, which if used invariably provoked a fight, and since E.B. stood six feet four, two inches taller than Anais' father, the initials stood.

For her wedding E.B. had given Julia a large holding of negotiable bonds so that she and Arthur could have a good start, and because he made it a rule never to give to one girl without giving to the other, he had given Anais his house on Sutton Place. His words had been, "Hell, I never liked New York, so what do I need a house here for?" And he reasoned that Julia and Arthur would be moving to London with Arthur's firm, and Anais would need something special so that she would not miss Julia so much, and he and his wife, Cora, moved lock, stock, and barrel back to Dallas.

Anais' father's voice was distant as it came over the phone.

"Well, don't worry about it, honey," he said as he tapped his fingers rhythmically on the mahogany desk in tune with the thoughts that were running through his head. After he said good-bye to Anais, he buzzed his secretary and asked her to get E.B. on the phone.

The telephone rang instantly after Anais hung up. It was Adelaide.

"Hi," she said with a lilt in her voice. "Can you meet me for lunch?"

"Love to," Anais said without hesitation.

They met at a little French restaurant on Fifty-sixth Street between Fifth Avenue and Avenue of the Americas, which was one of their favorites.

The room had overhead globes and the tables were covered with red-and-white-checkered cloths. The chairs were simple dark wood restaurant chairs. It was not elegant but very enchanting.

Their favorite waiter, André, greeted them at the entrance. After so many years André always seemed to remain the same. He had waited on them throughout their adolescence and his French charm had always made them giggle, and as grown women he still made them giggle with his gift of flattery.

André led them to their favorite table in the corner near the window that was curtained in the same red-and-white-checkered fabric, hung from brass rings around a shiny brass rod.

André brought them each a glass of wine. He sighed and said, "At least it's not Coca-Cola anymore." They smiled up at him with bright eyes, which always pleased André.

Lunch was served and André left them to wait on others. Despite the humble appearance of the restaurant, it was very popular with those who knew the best establishments.

Adelaide searched Anais' face carefully and decided that Anais looked well, just a little tense.

"I've been a little concerned about you, you know," she finally said.

"Oh!" Anais said innocently.

"Anais, I have known you for a long time. Give me

some credit for observance. You haven't been the same since Rome. Why can't you talk to me about it? We've always shared everything, haven't we?" Adelaide asked in earnest.

"Of course we have and it's nothing that won't pass." Anais lowered her eyes.

"Anais, I don't think it's that simple, and there's no need to keep it pent up, since I guessed long ago, my dear." Adelaide looked at Anais with concern flooding her eyes as tears brimmed in Anais'. "I'm very fond of Gathen, and I love you. I want you to know that when you're ready to talk, I'm here."

Anais touched Adelaide's hand softly and said, "Thank you, Adelaide. I will eventually." She sniffled gently.

"Good. Now that that's said, let's eat."

The glad tidings of Christmas spread over the city in a spectrum of bright colors, infecting everyone with its joy. Shoppers hurried along Fifth Avenue, trying for once not to be caught doing last-minute shopping.

Church bells chimed Christmas carols through the streets as soft snow flurries began to fall, dusting pedestrians with brief sparkles.

All over the world, businessmen and diplomats were wrapping up deals of corporations and countries in order to be home at Christmas. Those who were getting older could not believe that Christmas was here again, and to those whose years were few in number, it had at last arrived. It was time to lay aside the woes of everyday life and reach out to touch the magic of the season. Anais imagined that Arthur was making plans to finish his business so that he could be home with Andy for Christmas.

Anais stepped through the doors of Saks Fifth Avenue onto the side street across from St. Patrick's Cathedral. The sable cossack hat that she wore caught the glittering snowflakes as she walked toward Fifth Avenue. She carried brightly wrapped Christmas gifts under her arms. She averted her eyes from the fast-falling snow. When she looked up again, Gathen was standing before her. In spite of the cold, he wore only a tweed jacket with a silk scarf hanging around his neck and soft leather gloves.

"Hello, Anais," he said softly.

"Gathen!" She caught her breath, and with as much composure as she could muster, she said, "It's so good to see you."

"You, too," he said, but the sad look in his eyes said much more.

"How have you been?" he asked without his eyes ever wavering from their melancholy stare.

"Very well. And you?"

"Well, I suppose." He smiled down at her and she felt a shiver go through her body. "You look lovely," he said.

Anais looked at him and their eyes fixed for a moment and they both knew that the love they felt for each other still remained as strong as it had ever been. He reached for her packages.

"Which direction are you walking?" he asked as she released the boxes to him.

"To Fifty-seventh Street," she replied.

"Good. I'm heading that way. I'll walk with you," he said.

Anais looked at Gathen's attire and asked, "Aren't you cold?"

"No," he said, "just lonely."

"Oh, Gathen, don't," she pleaded.

"Then I'm not cold." He teased her with his eyes.

"I received the magnolia. Thank you very much."

"I have a friend who grows things." He smiled at her again.

They walked close together, their arms sometimes touching. They strolled slowly through the rushing throng of people, each dreading their approach to Tiffany's. There was so much to be said and so little time.

The yellow light from the shopwindows reflected against the dancing flakes as they made a shadowy descent to the ground, forming glittering drifts along the gutter and in corners.

When they reached Fifty-seventh Street, Gathen glanced at the stylishly decorated Tiffany window and said, "I would like to buy a gift for you, but I know you won't allow me to." He looked at her with a sad smile in his eyes.

"No, you mustn't. This was my gift, meeting you this evening," she said.

Gathen put a firmer grip on Anais' packages and looked at her with a twinkle in his eyes.

"Then may I ask you to give me a small Christmas gift?" Anais regarded him with questioning eyes and a tiny smile touched one corner of her lips and she answered, "What is it?"

"Will you stop for a few minutes and have a drink with me?"

"Good. I will bring," Helga said, leaving the room. Anais gazed long into the yellow crackling flames and her mind wandered back to the house in the country in Italy.

Helga soon returned with a tray and placed it on the mahogany table in front of the fire. Helga's return drew Anais back from her thoughts with a start. She looked up quickly, as if Helga might have been able to read her mind.

"Oh! Helga, you startled me." Anais laughed, somewhat disoriented by her silliness. She sat down on the sofa in front of the tray. Helga busily put things in place and chatted away while she did so.

"When Mr. Carlyle and Mr. Barclay were here last week with some gentlemen, they did not want me to serve them, just cook and clean up the dishes. Didn't seem right having guests and making them do for themselves." Helga shook her head silently as if trying to bring something that was in the back of her mind to the forefront, but it kept eluding her. Anais could only stare at Helga in astonishment. Helga left the room with a puzzled look on her round face. Anais was even more puzzled, since Arthur was supposed to have been in Paraguay and Elliott in Montreal.

Anais sat on the side of her canopied bed looking as if she belonged in a bygone year, her smoky hair spread about the shoulders of the poet-sleeved white nightgown that had a blue silk ribbon running through the pleated yoke and a small border of lace on the collar.

The day had gone well as far as getting the Christmas decorations in order was concerned, but the puzzle of Elliott and Arthur was preying on her mind and refused to be dismissed by reasoning that Arthur certainly had access to the house—after all he had spent years here off and on with Julia. "But why not say so?" Her thoughts spoke out loud. He certainly had the opportunity and he had made no effort to see Andy.

Anais was still mulling these disturbing things in her mind when the wind began to rise and the trees lashed back and forth in a fury as the heavy clouds pelted the earth with huge drops of rain. Anais went quickly to pull the window down, when through the dark and swaying trees she caught a glimpse of light coming from the old cottage that was once used as a guesthouse; but guests now always stayed in the main house, unless someone wanted a complete retreat when they came to visit. The yellow light glowed briefly through the trees and went out.

Anais pressed her head against the post of the bed as she sat on the edge. She was, to say the least, a little frightened. She started to pick up the phone and call Karl, but decided against it. She looked at the clock: it was late and Karl would go to investigate and might get hurt. Anais went back to the window and peered out. There was only darkness. She left the window and got into bed.

She thought, "Could I have imagined the light? No, I did not," she concluded.

At eight o'clock the next morning, Anais went down to the kitchen, where she knew she would find Helga.

"Helga," Anais began without salutation, "is there any-one down at the guest cottage?"

"Why, no, Miss LaPrell. There's no one here but Karl and me. Why do you ask?" Helga asked, just as puzzled as Anais.

"I think I saw a light on down there last night," Anais said.

"The electricity is off. Been off a long time," Helga answered.

"I think I'll go down and have a look. Perhaps my imagination ran away with the storm." She smiled at Helga.

"Wait, I will call Karl. You can never tell—a vagrant might have wandered in out of the rain."

Anais waited at the back door for Karl, who came in heavy work boots and carrying a big stick.

Anais trekked over the soggy ground with the mud sometimes nearly covering the top of her shoes, which prompted Karl to say, "You should have worn some other shoes. I'll clean those when we get back." At that moment Karl's foot slipped into a deep mudhole and he swore discreetly under his breath as Anais helped him to extricate his foot.

Although the cottage was well kept it looked sad and abandoned. "We must do something about this cottage. It shouldn't just sit like this. Perhaps one of Adelaide's protégés could use it. It's rather a pretty little house," she said.

Karl took a key ring that held a jumble of keys and unlocked the door. It opened onto a charming sitting room that held a large porcelain stove that sat between two heavily curtained windows. Anais and Karl walked around the room carefully. Karl opened the door to the bedroom, where neatly made twin rosewood beds took up most of the room. Anais examined the bureau drawers and found nothing there. She went to the window and pulled the drapes back. There in the undergrowth were distinct automobile tracks. Broken branches hung from the bushes where the car had squeezed into the thicket. Anais called Karl to the window.

"Look, Karl, there has been someone here!" she said with excitement pitching her voice. Karl looked at the wheel marks with concern spreading in his pale-blue eyes. "I'd better call the police," he said.

The police arrived in about fifteen minutes. They walked around the grounds with Karl and Anais and searched the cottage and ascertained that nothing had been taken. One of the policemen said, "We try to patrol the place as often as we can, but sometimes they come in by the back road around the lake. The youngsters sort of use the place as a lovers' lane. We'll try to step up the patrol."

"Well, nice seeing you, Miss LaPrell." They touched the tips of their caps and got back into the patrol car. Anais and Karl watched the car back out and pull away. Somehow Anais' instinct ran contrary to that of the police, and she saw more to the intrusion than just young lovers looking for a place to be alone.

Anais stayed one more night. She went through the Christmas decorations with love and tenderness. Some of the ornaments dated back to before she and Julia were born. Anais held a shiny red ball up and the lamp played with the lights in it, and for a few moments through the little pinpoint of light Anais was ferried back through the passage of memory to the magic of childhood at Christmastime, where there were only small hurts that could be cured by a kiss from Mommy and Daddy.

Anais heard herself giggle as her father held her up so

that she could reach a branch to hang the shimmering red ball. Julia stood on the floor giggling through her fingers that were clasped tightly over her mouth for fear that Anais would drop the ornament. From the floor, where she sat surrounded by Christmas decorations, Anais could smell the fragrance of the fir tree and hear the bells of Christmas. She leaned back against the foot of the bed and dreamed of the past. It took a few moments before she realized that the Christmas bells was the telephone ringing. She hurried up to the phone and was surprised to hear Elliott's lighthearted voice say, "Darling, I didn't know you were going to the country."

When Anais arrived back at the house in New York, Tillie met her at the door and told her, "Your father wants you to call him right away. He said it's important." Tillie was noncommittal as she went back to what she had been doing before Anais came in.

"Is he downtown or at home?" Anais called to Tillie's disappearing back.

"Downtown," Tillie called back as she went through the door.

Anais went into the library and telephoned her father. She first reached his secretary, who put her through to her father immediately.

"Daddy, is there anything wrong?" she asked anxiously.

"Hello, honey. It's not serious. But do you remember the bonds your uncle gave Julia for a wedding present?"

"Yes," she replied still puzzled.

"Did Julia give them to you?" her father asked, and without waiting for an answer he continued: "E.B. says that he heard that they were floating on the market." He paused. "I was just wondering if you needed money."

"Why, no. I don't know anything about it. Is Uncle E.B. sure?"

E.B. was Anais' father's brother, and his Christian name was abbreviated to his initials because he could not stand his first name, which if used invariably provoked a fight, and since E.B. stood six feet four, two inches taller than Anais' father, the initials stood.

For her wedding E.B. had given Julia a large holding of negotiable bonds so that she and Arthur could have a good start, and because he made it a rule never to give to one girl without giving to the other, he had given Anais his house on Sutton Place. His words had been, "Hell, I never liked New York, so what do I need a house here for?" And he reasoned that Julia and Arthur would be moving to London with Arthur's firm, and Anais would need something special so that she would not miss Julia so much, and he and his wife, Cora, moved lock, stock, and barrel back to Dallas.

Anais' father's voice was distant as it came over the phone.

"Well, don't worry about it, honey," he said as he tapped his fingers rhythmically on the mahogany desk in tune with the thoughts that were running through his head. After he said good-bye to Anais, he buzzed his secretary and asked her to get E.B. on the phone.

The telephone rang instantly after Anais hung up. It was Adelaide.

"Hi," she said with a lilt in her voice. "Can you meet me for lunch?"

"Love to," Anais said without hesitation.

They met at a little French restaurant on Fifty-sixth Street between Fifth Avenue and Avenue of the Americas, which was one of their favorites.

The room had overhead globes and the tables were covered with red-and-white-checkered cloths. The chairs were simple dark wood restaurant chairs. It was not elegant but very enchanting.

Their favorite waiter, André, greeted them at the entrance. After so many years André always seemed to remain the same. He had waited on them throughout their adolescence and his French charm had always made them giggle, and as grown women he still made them giggle with his gift of flattery.

André led them to their favorite table in the corner near the window that was curtained in the same red-and-white-checkered fabric, hung from brass rings around a shiny brass rod.

André brought them each a glass of wine. He sighed and said, "At least it's not Coca-Cola anymore." They smiled up at him with bright eyes, which always pleased André.

Lunch was served and André left them to wait on others. Despite the humble appearance of the restaurant, it was very popular with those who knew the best establishments.

Adelaide searched Anais' face carefully and decided that Anais looked well, just a little tense.

"I've been a little concerned about you, you know," she finally said.

"Oh!" Anais said innocently.

"Anais, I have known you for a long time. Give me

some credit for observance. You haven't been the same since Rome. Why can't you talk to me about it? We've always shared everything, haven't we?" Adelaide asked in earnest.

"Of course we have and it's nothing that won't pass." Anais lowered her eyes.

"Anais, I don't think it's that simple, and there's no need to keep it pent up, since I guessed long ago, my dear." Adelaide looked at Anais with concern flooding her eyes as tears brimmed in Anais'. "I'm very fond of Gathen, and I love you. I want you to know that when you're ready to talk, I'm here."

Anais touched Adelaide's hand softly and said, "Thank you, Adelaide. I will eventually." She sniffled gently.

"Good. Now that that's said, let's eat."

The glad tidings of Christmas spread over the city in a spectrum of bright colors, infecting everyone with its joy. Shoppers hurried along Fifth Avenue, trying for once not to be caught doing last-minute shopping.

Church bells chimed Christmas carols through the streets as soft snow flurries began to fall, dusting pedestrians with brief sparkles.

All over the world, businessmen and diplomats were wrapping up deals of corporations and countries in order to be home at Christmas. Those who were getting older could not believe that Christmas was here again, and to those whose years were few in number, it had at last arrived. It was time to lay aside the woes of everyday life and reach out to touch the magic of the season. Anais imagined that Arthur was making plans to finish his business so that he could be home with Andy for Christmas.

Anais stepped through the doors of Saks Fifth Avenue onto the side street across from St. Patrick's Cathedral. The sable cossack hat that she wore caught the glittering snowflakes as she walked toward Fifth Avenue. She carried brightly wrapped Christmas gifts under her arms. She averted her eyes from the fast-falling snow. When she looked up again, Gathen was standing before her. In spite of the cold, he wore only a tweed jacket with a silk scarf hanging around his neck and soft leather gloves.

"Hello, Anais," he said softly.

"Gathen!" She caught her breath, and with as much composure as she could muster, she said, "It's so good to see you."

"You, too," he said, but the sad look in his eyes said much more.

"How have you been?" he asked without his eyes ever wavering from their melancholy stare.

"Very well. And you?"

"Well, I suppose." He smiled down at her and she felt a shiver go through her body. "You look lovely," he said.

Anais looked at him and their eyes fixed for a moment and they both knew that the love they felt for each other still remained as strong as it had ever been. He reached for her packages.

"Which direction are you walking?" he asked as she released the boxes to him.

"To Fifty-seventh Street," she replied.

"Good. I'm heading that way. I'll walk with you," he said.

Anais looked at Gathen's attire and asked, "Aren't you cold?"

"No," he said, "just lonely."

"Oh, Gathen, don't," she pleaded.

"Then I'm not cold." He teased her with his eyes.

"I received the magnolia. Thank you very much."

"I have a friend who grows things." He smiled at her again.

They walked close together, their arms sometimes touching. They strolled slowly through the rushing throng of people, each dreading their approach to Tiffany's. There was so much to be said and so little time.

The yellow light from the shopwindows reflected against the dancing flakes as they made a shadowy descent to the ground, forming glittering drifts along the gutter and in corners.

When they reached Fifty-seventh Street, Gathen glanced at the stylishly decorated Tiffany window and said, "I would like to buy a gift for you, but I know you won't allow me to." He looked at her with a sad smile in his eyes.

"No, you mustn't. This was my gift, meeting you this evening," she said.

Gathen put a firmer grip on Anais' packages and looked at her with a twinkle in his eyes.

"Then may I ask you to give me a small Christmas gift?" Anais regarded him with questioning eyes and a tiny smile touched one corner of her lips and she answered, "What is it?"

"Will you stop for a few minutes and have a drink with me?"

She hesitated for a moment, fearing that too much time spent with Gathen would be detrimental to all of her resolutions, just when she was learning to live with them.

"All right, and since it will be my Christmas gift to you, I would like that very much."

They walked over to Park Avenue and somewhere in the low Sixties they came upon an old-fashioned pub with beveled glass doors that opened into a room that was dimly lighted with chandeliers of the Gay Nineties with dark ceiling fans spaced between them. A thick green palm plant stood against the wall and small tables covered with white cloths glowed in the faint light of the candles that sat in the center of them.

A waiter greeted them and showed them to a table in a secluded corner. When they were seated, the waiter helped Anais remove her coat and spread it over the back of the chair. She removed her hat and her dark hair fell freely around her face and she glowed like a Rembrandt painting with the yellow light of the candle dancing in her eyes. She looked down at the white tablecloth and traced the shadowy pattern of the candle with her finger. She knew that Gathen was watching her. When she did raise her eyes, his eyes were fixed on her. He looked at her filled with love.

He broke the silence and said, "Did you ever marvel at the gift of love?" Without giving her a chance to reply, he put his arms resolutely on the table and folded his hands together. He leaned toward her; the candlelight played with the shadows on his face and glinted in his eyes, setting them on fire. "How it casts aside gloom and doubt and gives the soul the power to soar, making everything right with the world. The good Lord made it so simple, Anais, and what I can't understand is why people make it so complicated." He leaned back in his chair and changed the subject abruptly, asking, "When is the wedding?"

"We have never set a date." Anais became stiff and upright. She clasped her hands together tightly on the table and was saved any further remarks on the wedding by the opportune appearance of the waiter asking if they were ready to order. His arrival ended any more talk of the wedding and Anais was more than grateful to him.

Gathen turned toward the door, where rainbows of light played up and down the beveled glass in the door as customers went in and out.

"I've always liked the snow," he mused.

"Oh, so have I. Whenever the first snowfall came, Julia and I would always wrap up, put our boots on, and go for a long walk. We did that every year for years, whether it was night or day." Anais smiled at the memory of times gone by.

"Julia?" Gathen asked.

"Julia was my sister. She died a few years ago." The words still brought pain to Anais.

"I am so sorry," Gathen said with genuine sympathy.

"Yes, we all were," Anais said quietly.

The waiter returned with their drinks; he placed Anais' glass of white wine before her and Gathen's scotch and soda before him and moved away so that they could continue their conversation.

Gathen raised his glass to Anais and said, "To you," and his eyes remained on her over the rim of his glass. He put the glass down and smiled at her. "Forgive me for staring

at you, but you see I don't know when I will see you again."

Anais lowered her head and said, "Gathen, you're breaking my heart."

His stare became cold for a moment and he said, "I would never do that, Anais; you're breaking your own heart."

If the waiter had not appeared again to ask if they cared for another drink, Anais would have broken into inconsolable sobbing, but at the sound of his voice she brought herself upright and her emotions under control. She took in a breath and said in a hollow voice, "I must go home now."

She looked at Gathen in despair and he held her gaze for a moment, then signaled the waiter, who appeared quickly at the table.

They left the warmth of the pub and walked out into the cold soft falling snow. Gathen returned Anais' Christmas boxes to her and turned the collar of his jacket up and looked at the drifting snow.

"Would you like me to get a taxi for you?" he asked.

"No, thank you. I'd like to walk."

He smiled at her and said, "First snowfall?"

"Something like that." She smiled back at him. Suddenly without warning, he took her by the shoulders and with her arms filled with her Christmas packages, Gathen kissed her hard on the lips.

"Merry Christmas, Anais," he said. Her eyes filled with tears and she turned and walked away. She looked back once and found Gathen still standing, watching her. A veil of snow flurries wrapped her in a misty white cloud and she vanished from his sight. Gathen turned and walked in the opposite direction toward Carnegie Hall.

As he walked through the falling snow, he banged his fist in his hand and thought, "It wasn't meant to be this way, Anais."

A curious feeling came over Anais as she let herself into the dimly lit entrance hall. There was something wrong, and she could not put her finger on just what it was, but she felt a dark specter that swam about her like murky waters. She removed her hat in front of the ornate gilt mirror in the drawing room. She stared back at herself from the mirror: her golden eyes looked sad and haunted, and she wished there was something she could do to erase that look. She rubbed her fingers across her eyes in a vain attempt at restoring a hint of light back into their lifeless state. It didn't help, and she turned to the window and watched the snow that was now blowing in gusts over the lawn which sloped down to the river. It was so green in summer, and now it was a white carpet glowing against the dark rushing waters. Anais had turned the lights out when she went to gaze out of the window in an effort to instill some peace in her mind from the silent dancing snow.

"What are you doing in the dark, Anais?" Tillie asked from the doorway.

"Just watching the snow," Anais answered.

"Your uncle E.B. called. He'll be up for Christmas. They're going to stay at your folks' until all of you go up to Connecticut."

A big smile came over Anais' face and her eyes brightened suddenly at the thought of spending Christmas with her uncle again.

"The gathering of the clan," Tillie said tersely. "Now with all those expensive presents, it would be nice if someone remembered what the meaning of the day was." Tillie was still thoughtful. "You know, Anais, it's funny your uncle coming up for Christmas; he hasn't come up in years for the holidays."

"No, but it will be nice having the family together, won't it?"

"Yeah, I suppose so." Tillie was not as enthusiastic as Anais. For one thing, Uncle E.B. spoiled Andy rotten and he was very hard to live with for a few weeks afterward: every piece of furniture was one of Uncle E.B.'s horses from the great Bell Ranch.

"Did you finish your shopping?" Tillie asked Anais.

"Just about; and you?" They both gazed out at the falling snow. There was an uneasiness in both of the women and neither wanted to say anything that would bring it to the surface, because neither of them knew what it was. Anais knew that it was not just her ceaseless love for Gathen; it was something else.

"D'you know . . ." Tillie started to say something, then thought better of it and instead said, "Would you like to eat now?"

"No, thank you. I think I'll just go to my room. I'm a bit tired."

As Anais started out of the door with her Christmas bundles, the telephone rang.

"I'll get it," Tillie said. She lifted the receiver and said, "Oh, how are you, Mr. Barclay?" with even less enthusiasm than she had had when she heard that Uncle E.B. was coming.

Tillie handed the phone to Anais and left the room.

"How are you, darling?" Whatever enthusiasm Anais showed was dragged up from the depths of her being. It was an effort and no longer came naturally.

After her conversation with Elliott and in the solitude of her room, Anais reflected upon her life with Elliott and tried to find the point in their relationship when she stopped loving him. It had been before she met Gathen in Rome. Falling in love with Gathen had only been easier because she did not have a love. She had forgotten that love was exciting and made you want to sing with joy. When she was alone she would often daydream of love—until she met Gathen. It was no longer that way with Elliott.

Elliott was devoted to her, and his parents and her parents thought of each as a part of their family.

They had met one summer when her parents had rented a beautiful old house from a friend for the summer in Bridgehampton. She and Elliott had been in their teens with all the innocence of adolescence. They went to the movies, ate bags of popcorn; they spent that summer sailing and swimming, doing all the things that young lovers do. Elliott was so handsome with his dark hair and blue eyes. His one fault was that he was unaccepting of people who were different. He was an unrelenting snob and often made unkind remarks about people whom he did not consider his social equal. But to Anais he was kind, attentive, and charming. Anais lay on the bed and placed her hands behind her head as she mulled over Elliott, and somehow Julia and Arthur kept finding their way into her thoughts. Julia had not met Arthur that summer; it was later when she went off to Radcliffe, where Anais and Adelaide joined her a year later.

When Anais and Adelaide arrived as freshmen at Radcliffe, Julia had already met Arthur. He was in his last year at Harvard Business School. Arthur was on full scholarship and did not have the time nor the money to keep up with some of his fellow students. He was usually busy studying and was very conscientious about it. Anais had found Arthur's manners rather affected; other than that he seemed nice enough, but Anais often wondered what Julia had thought of him. Once, when his father came to visit him on campus, the presence of the old man obviously embarrassed Arthur, with his work worn hands from the hard labor at the steel mill. Anais remembered, when Arthur finally introduced them, the strong grip of his big hand as it swallowed hers. There was a genuine feeling of warmth that cut across the barrier of money: there was instant liking and respect, and Anais could tell that he was a good man and would have sacrificed everything so that his son could have the best.

He left suddenly, without saying good-bye to anyone. Arthur made excuses, but Anais knew that the old man had too much pride to cause his son any further embarrassment. When Julia and Arthur married, he had been sent an invitation, but he did not come to the wedding. He did send a letter, carefully written by someone else, wishing them happiness, but at that particular time they were very busy at the mill and he could not get away. And when Andy was born, he sent another letter saying, "Take care of that grandson of mine," but he never saw Andy. Julia sent him pictures of Andy in different stages of growth. Then one day they received word that he had died. Anais could only wonder if indeed Arthur had not been relieved at the news, and he would no longer be reminded of his background.

The snow muffled the noises of the city and blurred it in a ghostly veil as it brushed against the window, locking her in troubled thoughts.

When Anais awakened in the morning the sky was a pewter gray and the snow was still falling. The Fifty-ninth Street Bridge was decorated with mounds of fluffy snow piled on its dark spires, and traffic crawled across it at a snail's pace. Anais dressed in a woolen skirt, sweater, boots, and a fur coat. She left the house early to visit her mother and to take Andy to the park. She knew he would be bursting with excitement at the big snowfall. It was already the seventeenth of December and they would soon leave for the country, which would be even more fun for him.

Anais was let in by a very proper Rose, who was not in the least like Tillie, but Rose did not wield the same power as Tillie. She told Anais that her mother was in the living room. Anais thanked her and went off to join her mother. When she opened the door, the room was in shadows and she only saw the fire burning, and she was completely taken by surprise when she saw a man of six feet four with silver hair standing before the fireplace.

"Uncle E.B.!" she exclaimed with delight. "I didn't know that you had arrived." She ran to him and he squeezed her in his big arms.

"How's my sugar?" he asked, laughing.

E.B. and his wife, Cora, had never had children, so Anais was a special delight to them. She was just as much their little girl as she was to her parents. They shared their love for her, as she shared her love for them, and everyone was pleased with the whole situation.

"Uncle E.B., you didn't tell me you were coming so soon," Anais admonished him gently.

"We wanted to surprise you," her aunt Cora said, coming through the door. Anais went to her aunt and they embraced lovingly.

Unlike the other LaPrells, Aunt Cora was a fiery redhead with sharp green eyes. She was not a beauty, but she had her own style, which at times is far more elegant than the most physically beautiful of women. Her mouth was wide and painted a bright red and, like most redheads, she was freckled all over. She stood tall and erect.

"I believe this is going to be one of our happiest Christmases," Anais said. "Andy is going to be simply wild."

"I thought, Anais, that we might go up to the country a few days earlier, now that Cora and E.B. are here," her mother said.

"Marvelous idea. We don't see that much snow down in Dallas," Aunt Cora said. "But first, Anais, we have to do some shopping. I haven't been shopping in New York in ages."

"You and Cora go ahead; E.B. and I'll pick Andy up from school. We've got some man things to do," her father said.

"Well, get your things, Aunt Cora. Are you coming, Mother?" Anais asked, picking up her coat.

"No, darling, I have some other things to do. You and Cora run along. Have fun," her mother said, leaving the room.

After Anais and Cora had left, Anais' mother came back into the drawing room, and with a troubled voice said, "I'll pick Andy up from school and take him to Anais'." She looked at the clock on the table. "They should be arriving soon."

In the distance E.B. and Anais' father heard the doorbell and shortly afterward Rose appeared in the doorway with two men. They were tall with somber eyes that were keenly alert and seemed to dart back and forth in their boldly masculine faces. After shaking hands with Anais' father and E.B., they were introduced to her mother.

"I believe that I will leave you gentlemen. Rose will bring some coffee in." She bowed her head slightly. "Good day, gentlemen."

"Nice to have met you, Mrs. LaPrell," the two men said.

As the door closed behind her, Mrs. LaPrell heard one of the men say, "I can understand your concern, sir. In our investigations . . ." The door shut on the words and Anais' mother heaved a deep worried sigh as she collected her coat from the hall closet. The cold snow that stung her delicate face as she walked from the apartment building to the waiting limousine did not compare to the cold chill that ran through her heart.

The yellow taxi pulled up behind the shining black limousine that waited in front of Anais' house. Anais and Cora got out, loaded with bundles and laughing like guilty schoolgirls who were getting away with a secret escapade.

The taxi driver helped them to the door and left with a generous tip.

"You know, Anais, I have a good mind to leave some of these things here so that your uncle E.B. won't find out the kind of woman he's married." Aunt Cora snickered and wrinkled her nose.

"You might have a point; you went wild in Bergdorf's," Anais said, pushing the door open with her foot.

"Hi, Anais," Andy greeted them at the door. His cheeks were red from the cold. Anais bent and kissed him.

"You've been playing in the snow."

"Yeah, with Timothy," he said, rushing to hug his aunt Cora.

Aunt Cora put all of her bundles on the floor, where she stood and caught Andy in her arms.

"How's my big man?" Aunt Cora said.

"There you two are," Anais' mother said from the doorway. Tillie stood behind her; they had been in deep discussion when they heard Anais and Cora come in. "I've been waiting to take you back, Cora. Timothy can put those things into the car. Rose is waiting dinner. Andy, get your things now; Grandpa and Uncle E.B. are waiting for you." Her mother seemed anxious, and Anais went to her and said softly, "Is there anything wrong, Mother?" Her mother patted her on the hand and said, "No, dear, just a little headache and Andy and I have been waiting, that's all." She gave Anais a fleeting glance that still held a troubled look.

Anais and Tillie watched them get into the car from the window.

"Do you know what's troubling Mother?" she asked Tillie.

"No, I don't," Tillie said. "But something sure is."

They gathered up the gaily wrapped packages that did not match either of their moods and put them into the closet with the rest of the Christmas gifts.

CHAPTER 9

Slush spewed from the wheels of the BMW as it sped along the parkway. Anais sat behind the wheel with a disgruntled Tillie beside her. The snow had stopped and the late-morning sun flooded the white land as shadows from the bare branches of the trees danced on the untouched snow.

"You know, Anais," Tillie said after a long period of silence, "I have a feeling in my bones that something is wrong. I can't put my finger on anything in particular, but it's bothering me to death." Tillie twirled her thumbs aimlessly.

"I have the same feelings. I can't get it out of my mind that whoever it was that was in the cottage, was not there for a lovers' rendezvous." Anais had told Tillie about the light in the cottage, but she had not told Tillie about Arthur and Elliott being at the house in the country. It was something that she could not explain, and Tillie would certainly want a reasonable explanation.

"And something else: your uncle E.B. hasn't been up here for Christmas in years. I know he comes on business and spoils Andy so that nobody can live with him for weeks afterward, but he's as nervous as a kitten. And your aunt Cora's busy shopping and pretending to be having just one carefree time of it. And your mother is listless with worry." Tillie and Anais were finally speaking out loud things that had been filling their thoughts for too long a time now.

"I promise," Anais said with determination, "we'll get to the bottom of this. We certainly can't go on living with whatever"—Anais threw one hand in the air—"this is."

"Yeah. It's beginning to get to me," Tillie snorted.

By the time Anais and Tillie reached the house, clouds were beginning to cluster and the sun was now just a pale ball shrouded behind a gray translucent haze.

When the car pulled into the driveway, Anais' father appeared with Andy and Uncle E.B. Uncle E.B. and Anais' father were both dressed in heavy plaid wool hunting jackets, and Andy wore a dark-blue snowsuit and bright-red rubber boots. Snow clung to every piece of clothing that he wore: he romped and rolled in every snow mound he could find.

"Hello, my little snowman," Anais called to him.

The three of them approached the car to help the women with their bundles. Anais' father looked up at the fading sun and said, "Looks like you and Tillie just made it. I think we're in for some more snow."

"Yippee-ee," Andy shouted with glee. Uncle E.B. put his arm around Andy's shoulder to quiet him gently.

"The tree's up, Anais, but Grandma said that we were to wait for you and Tillie before we started to put the balls on."

"Oh, good, darling, because I love decorating the tree. We'll start after dinner."

"Good. That means that I can stay up late," Andy said, pleased.

"Well, a little later." Anais smiled at him.

"Come on, Tillie, I want to show you the tree," and he pulled Tillie by the hand toward the house. Both Anais' father and Uncle E.B. turned and watched them disappear into the house. A swift glance passed between the two men, and Uncle E.B. turned and his big frame moved rather hurriedly for no apparent reason in the direction of the house. Anais' father opened the back door of the car and started to gather the bundles to be carried into the house.

Tillie was delighted with the tree as Andy pointed out all of its fine qualities and its superiority over the other trees in the woods, and he was very pleased to have helped in cutting down his Christmas tree.

Tillie always spent Christmas with her sister in Pennsylvania, but the uneasy feeling that she felt in her bones compelled her to stay close to Anais, though she was going to feel like an odd thumb. This was Karl and Helga's domain, and there would be precious little for her to do around the house, but Tillie decided to endure this discomfort for the sake of her own peace of mind.

When Anais joined her mother and Cora in the living room, where a bright fire burned and crackled in the fireplace, and the burning logs and the thick unadorned fir tree fragranced the room, Anais was surprised to find Adelaide with Cora and her mother.

"When did you get up?" Anais asked Adelaide.

"Last night. Jim got back earlier than he thought, so we just decided to unwind in the country for a while." Adelaide flashed a bright smile. "You know the Merriwether place near me? Well, it's been up for sale for quite a while. It's part of an estate settlement and the heirs were becoming anxious, so they've settled for what they could get. It's a lovely old house, fifteen acres and that beautiful lake. Yes, Gathen has gotten himself a very good buy," Adelaide said, very pleased indeed.

Anais was caught by complete surprise at this bit of news, and was first tempted to cry out. Instead she only said softly, "How nice," as Adelaide went on.

"The house is completely furnished, so Gathen is going to spend Christmas in it. This is going to be a better Christmas than I had thought. It's so nice, having all the people that you are fond of around at Christmas."

"Yes, it is," Anais said with sincerity.

"Will you come over for cocktails this evening?" Adelaide asked, preparing to leave.

"We're going to decorate the tree tonight. Perhaps tomorrow," Anais said.

"Good. Gathen won't be up for a few days yet. I'm sure he'll want you to see the house," Adelaide said.

"That would be lovely, Adelaide," Anais' mother broke in. "It's nice to visit all the neighbors during the holidays. And I am sure Cora and E.B. would love to meet our new neighbor."

"I'll walk you to the car," Anais said coolly to Adelaide.

As they stepped out of the door a few flurries of snowflakes were beginning to fall. Anais said to Adelaide, "Whose idea was it for Gathen to buy a house up here?"

"Darling, it was his own idea. I only introduced him to the music world. He makes his own decisions and lives his own life. I am a friend of his, not an adviser. He saw the house from the road and liked it. I merely said that it was for sale. He looked at it and bought it. Tell me, now, what was I supposed to say?" Adelaide looked at Anais with a scowl between her lovely raised eyebrows.

"I know, Adelaide, it's just very difficult," Anais said apologetically.

"It will all work out, Anais, for whatever is best." Adelaide kissed her on the cheek and got into the car.

"Get home safely," Anais called to Adelaide as she drove away.

After dinner, boxes of Christmas-tree decorations were brought into the living room, and everyone began picking out his favorite ornaments to hang on the tree. The fire glowed softly from the fireplace, and outside snow was falling, as it should be for this festive season. There was peace and love in this quiet family setting, protected from the harsh cold outside by a beautiful, comfortable house, and all should have been well, as the laughter of a child filled the house with his joy and expectations.

The tall full-branched tree that almost touched the high ceiling was now completely trimmed; beautiful terra-cotta angels that were hand painted and dressed in silk and gold robes hung from dark branches. They were the pride of Anais' mother, who had bought them in Italy years ago, and they matched the crèche that stood under the tree.

"Turn on the lights! Turn on the lights!" Andy cried.

Aunt Cora turned the lamps out and Anais turned the tree lights on. Everyone gasped as tiny colored bulbs flickered on and off, casting huge spiny shadows across the ceiling.

"Look, Tillie," Andy said, pointing to the ceiling.

"It's beautiful, honey," Tillie said, giving the excited little boy a big hug.

Everyone admired the tree while sipping coffee. Andy had a cup of hot chocolate, then it was his bedtime. The lights were turned off on the tree and everyone decided to turn in.

Anais and Tillie put Andy to bed and went to their rooms. Tillie's room was next to Andy's, while Anais' was farther down the hall. Her parents shared the room across from Andy, and Uncle E.B. and Aunt Cora shared the room on the other side of Andy.

Anais climbed into bed and watched the embers burning out in her fireplace. She left her curtains opened so that she could watch the falling snow. She fell asleep somewhere between watching the snow and listening to the dropping embers as they slipped through the grating.

Deep into the night Anais stirred quietly in her sleep. She turned over and came out of her sleep. She thought she had heard something. She listened for a moment but there was nothing but silence. She cushioned her head on her arm to try to resume sleep again, which of late she found a much more comfortable state to be in. She raised her head and pushed her hair back in an effort to hear better. She raised up on her elbows. There were muffled voices coming from under her window. Anais got up to look out. It was snowing very hard now and she could only see shadows of figures in the dark. Anais recognized her father and her uncle, but she could not recognize the third man, who seemed to be carrying a rifle over his shoulder.

Anais thought that perhaps her father and uncle had confronted a hunter on the property. She quickly put on a pair of trousers and a warm woolen coat, slipped on boots without stockings, and hurried downstairs.

"Daddy! Uncle E.B.!" she called in a whisper.

Her father rushed to her and said, "What the devil are you doing down here, Anais?"

"I heard you and Uncle E.B. down here. Who was that man?"

As Anais had come through the door, the man had quickly disappeared into the thickets.

"There was no other man here. Now go back to bed before you catch a cold," her father said, leading her back through the door. "E.B. and I were talking a little business and decided to come out for some air. I didn't know we'd wake up the whole damn house," her father said, not at all convincingly to Anais.

"I was sure I saw another man with you and Uncle E.B., with something over his shoulder. There's no one hunting here, I hope."

"There was no one here. For God's sake, Anais, go back to bed. The house is cold." Her father spoke more sharply to her than she could ever remember. He seemed extremely on edge and Uncle E.B. offered her no solace. Uncle E.B. had always come to her defense if she was being made to do something that she did not wish to do. He would at least say, "Let her stay if she wants to." This time he just stood back in the shadows with both hands buried deep in his trousers pockets, his big frame shifting uneasily from foot to foot.

Anais went back to her room, even more disturbed now than before, because her father and Uncle E.B. were acting as strangely as her mother, though Aunt Cora showed no outward signs of anxiety.

When Anais arrived back in her room she again looked out of her window, but there was nothing except the soft patter of the snow falling into the bushes. There were circles of footprints that the snow was quickly erasing.

Anais went to Tillie's door and knocked softly. She heard Tillie's voice, muffled with sleep, say, "Come in."

Tillie turned on the lamp beside her bed and reached for her robe. She blinked her eyes in an attempt to adjust them to the electric light. "What's the matter, Anais?" She sat up in bed, her eyes, searching Anais' face, looked very worried.

"Tillie, I just saw a man with a rifle over his shoulder talking to Daddy and Uncle E.B. under my window."

"Well, if they were talking to him they must know him," Tillie said, with a what-of-it? tone in her voice.

"They denied that there was anyone there with them. I have a feeling, Tillie, that whatever's going on, they're keeping it hidden from me, and I just don't know what it is. In the morning, Tillie, I want you to go with me down to the guest cottage."

Tillie and Anais were the first to rise; only Helga was up and about getting things ready for breakfast. Coffee perked merrily in the old-fashioned pot on the stove. Helga poured them each a cup.

"The buns are not quite ready, but soon," she assured them.

"We'll have some when we come back," Anais said, putting her cup down.

Anais and Tillie stepped out into a magical world of white. Snow was piled on the branches of the trees and they looked as if they could not hold another crystal flake, and the snow was still falling. Tillie looked up at the sky and said, "It's nice to have a white Christmas, but, Lord, I think you're overdoing it."

The two women trudged through the deep snow with very high steps in a great effort to keep their footing. They were rapidly being covered by the snow and would have looked like any bush if they had not kept moving.

When they reached the cottage they found the snow around it untouched by either humans or animals. They made their way up to the door and pushed it open. It looked the same as the day Anais and Karl had left it.

"What did you expect to find?" Tillie asked.

"I don't know, perhaps some evidence that someone might have been staying here." She looked around the sitting room while Tillie looked around the bedroom.

"At least it's warm in here," Anais said, brushing some of the snow from her hat. She turned to Tillie with a quizzical look on her face. "Warm?" She went to the ceramic stove and touched it carefully.

"Tillie, this stove is warm. Someone has been staying here."

"You're right," Tillie said, feeling the side of the stove.

Tillie and Anais took their boots and coats off in the mud room and joined the rest of the family in the breakfast room.

"Darling, you've been out already?" her mother greeted Anais as she kissed her mother on the cheek.

"Yes. Tillie and I went for a walk."

"That was very brave of both of you," her mother said with a little wry humor as she took a bite of Helga's honey bun. "Sit down, dear, and have your breakfast."

"Where's Daddy?" Anais asked.

"In the living room with Andy. They've had their breakfast."

Anais put her napkin down on the table and got up again. "I want to speak to Daddy for a moment." She left the table before her mother could question her.

Anais found her father and Andy admiring the Christmas tree. The lights were on and blinking away, to Andy's delight.

"Good morning, hon," her father said, looking up at her from the floor.

"Daddy, may I speak to you for a moment?" she asked, moving away from Andy. Her father followed her and asked, "What's up?"

"I think someone has been staying in the guest cottage."

Her father gave a look of genuine surprise and said, "I'd better call the sheriff then."

"Yes, I think so," she replied.

"You go back and have your breakfast, and I'll get to it right away."

When Anais left the room her father stood for a moment and rubbed his chin, trying to think of something. He reached for the telephone and said, "Sam, get someone over here. Yeah . . . okay. See you in a while." He hung up the telephone and went to the window to watch the falling snow, but his mind was far from the snow.

This thing would soon come to a climax and he did not want Anais getting in the way. It would be too dangerous and she was becoming too curious.

Almost an hour later there was the sound of feet stomping off clinging snow at the front door. Andy had retired with Helga and Karl to the kitchen, where the smell of a cake baking in the stove was holding his attention.

Anais' father had answered the doorbell and he took the two men into the library, where Uncle E.B. was waiting. Anais heard the bell and was on her way to the door, but her father had headed her off with a call that he had it, and when she approached them, he had let her know that he wanted to talk to the men alone with her uncle.

Anais was used to this; there were always certain things that her father handled without her and her mother, but she felt that this time she was the only one left out, and whatever it was had made her mother very nervous.

After her father's rebuff, Anais went to her room and picked up a book to read, but she found herself only looking at the print. When she heard the men leave, Anais went downstairs to ask her father about the visitors, and he answered, "Those were some men from the sheriff's office. They're going to check the place out and see what's going on," he said confidently.

"Oh," was Anais' only reply. Theirs was a small community and she knew all of the men from the sheriff's office; even if one was new, she certainly would have recognized one of the others.

Anais decided not to question her father any further. He did not want her to know and he meant not to tell her.

Anais found her mother, Aunt Cora, and Tillie all cozily ensconced in her mother's room.

"Ohh! Wait, Anais," Aunt Cora cried as Anais entered the room. Anais quickly covered her eyes with her hands and said, "I'm not looking."

Aunt Cora put the box that she had been wrapping down beside the bed and said, "It's all right now. You can take your hands away from your eyes."

"Is it pretty?" Anais asked.

"You'll see on Christmas morning," her aunt said.

"Only a few more days. Christmas comes and goes so quickly now," Anais said.

"It's called getting on in years. One day you're young" —Aunt Cora made a sweep with her hand—"and then suddenly you're not. So one must compensate for the acceleration of time by living every moment and not wasting time on the past." Aunt Cora looked toward the window with its sheer crisscross curtains. Her mother went to the fireplace and stirred the logs.

"Do you suppose we will be able to get to Adelaide's? It's still snowing." Her mother's gaze followed Cora's out of the window.

"Karl's cleared the driveway to the road, and the road's always kept cleared," Anais said.

Tillie, who had been very quiet through most of the conversation, spoke with a mind that seemed to be elsewhere: "It might stop soon."

At five o'clock Tillie watched from the window with

Andy as Anais, with her mother and father and uncle and aunt, climbed into the station wagon and started out for Adelaide's house. Tillie had now taken on the same nervous and worried look that Anais' mother wore.

"Come on, Andy, let's go up to my room and I'll read a story to you. You go on up and find what you want. I'll be up in a minute."

"Okay!" Andy said happily and ran up the steps.

Tillie went to the front door and opened it. Shortly a tall black man wearing a duffle coat and a navy woolen watch cap entered the door. He was covered with snow and wore heavy woolen gloves and boots.

"Ma'am," was his only greeting to Tillie. He consulted his watch, and in doing so, he shifted slightly the rifle that was strung across his shoulder.

"We'll be ready to move out at eight sharp. Be ready." He gave Tillie a small crooked smile of assurance when he heard Andy call to her. He opened the door and slipped out into the dark white evening.

Tillie watched the closed door for a moment, wringing her hands. She heard Andy run to the top of the steps; she looked up at the little boy and said, "Tillie's coming, honey."

Andy held his choice of book up to her. She looked at it and said, "We'll read for a little while. All right?"

Adelaide and her husband, Jim, greeted them at the door. Adelaide wore comfortable country clothes, a gray twin cashmere sweater set and a flannel gray skirt. They were all very casual country. Adelaide said, "I don't know why we all don't simply move to the country. It's so peaceful." She teased E.B. "You do know, E.B., that you don't have to wait until Christmas to pay us a visit."

"I always intend to come and see you, Adelaide, but concern it, I always seem to run out of time. But no more: you'll be first on my list and everything else will have to wait, you hear me?"

He put his big arms around Adelaide and she led them into the living room, where a fire burned in a huge stone fireplace, and the yellow flames reflected against a dark polished old wood-beamed ceiling. Crystal decanters sat on a low table in front of the fire, and vases were filled with yellow chrysanthemums. A Christmas tree touched the ceiling; white lights blinked on and off in sequence over silver decoration.

"Sit down, folks," Jim said, "and let's catch up on old times. First, what'll you have?" he asked, picking up one of the decanters.

"Bourbon and water for me," E.B. said.

"Scotch," Anais' father said, as if his mind had wandered for a moment.

"Ladies?" Jim asked.

"Same as E.B.," Cora said.

"I'll have a glass of sherry," Anais' mother said.

"I'll have a glass of sherry also," Anais said.

They settled back to enjoy the flavor of old friendship over a glass of spirits. The men enjoyed the intertwining of their conversation with the women, theirs being mostly of business and the women's mostly of Christmas shopping and Adelaide's patronage of the arts. During the conversation, E.B. said, "Cora almost broke me in those Fifth Avenue stores."

Aunt Cora looked modestly wronged and said, "E.B., how you exaggerate. My darling niece sitting over there can testify to my prudence."

Anais raised her eyes to the ceiling and said, "I certainly can, Aunt Cora."

Cora laughed and said to Anais, "Don't take that tone with your elders."

Anais' father looked at his watch and the festive spirit of Christmas left his eyes, and he said to Jim, "I'd like to speak to you for a moment, Jim, if you don't mind, in the library."

Jim got up and they excused themselves.

"You coming, E.B.?" Anais' father asked.

"Believe I will," E.B. said, getting up to follow them into the library.

"Will Elliott be coming soon?" Adelaide asked Anais.

"In a few days, I think," Anais replied.

"Ohh-hh! I got something for you, Anais, that you are going to simply love," Adelaide said. She could always without warning revert to adolescence. "What did you get me?"

"Wait and see." Anais smiled.

"Well, good folks"—Anais' father gave a quick glance at his watch again—"I think it's time we headed home."

As they did not wish to appear rude to the ladies, their private conversation in the library had lasted only about half an hour. They had rejoined the ladies and had spent the rest of the evening in small talk and local gossip with them.

Adelaide had reproached them when they returned from the library.

"Really! Must you all always discuss business, even at Christmas?"

Jim stroked her smooth chin and said playfully, "Do I ever say anything about your art doings?"

"That's different." Adelaide pouted.

The night wind had taken on a piercing chill and the snow was now hard little pellets that stung them in the face, and the first rush of air, as they stepped out into the night, took their breath away. The drive back was slow and though Christmas lights glimmered from windows and yards with outdoor decorated trees, the night had become unfriendly. The group rode back home in utter silence, as the headlights of the station wagon swept through dark and bare trees.

Lights burned from some of the windows, more as a beacon rather than a pronouncement that anyone was up and about in the house. No doubt Tillie and Andy were asleep, and Helga and Karl were in their cottage. The house looked warm and inviting as they rushed from the car into the house. Boots were discarded on a rubber mat in the corner and coats hung in the closet. Anais' father rubbed his hands together and said, "I think I need a stiff one. What about you, E.B.?" He smiled, but his lips bared his teeth in a grimace instead of the smile that he had intended.

"Sure thing," E.B. said agreeably.

"I think I'll check on Andy," Anais said. At that moment her mother walked into the room. Cora cast a sharp look of expectation on her face.

"I've just looked in on him," her mother said. "He's sound asleep and so is Tillie. I don't think there's any need to disturb him." She walked to the fireplace and warmed her hands.

"Would you pour a glass of brandy for me, dear?" she said to her husband.

He knelt before the fire and warmed the glass of brandy and took it to his wife, who had sat, rather pale, on the sofa next to Cora, whose elegantly painted cheeks were turning quite pale and belied her outward calmness.

Anais watched four nervous people and she thought, "Am I just imagining this? I haven't been exactly right lately." She sat in the wing chair and surveyed her family silently. Perhaps she was more upset than she had thought over her brief love affair with Gathen. Perhaps they were looking at her with more concern than she had realized, but she could not remember doing very much out of the ordinary; everyone becomes depressed now and then. She gazed into the yellow-and-blue flames that were licking up the chimney, and then cast secretive glances at her relatives.

"I'm going to make some coffee. Would anyone else like a cup?" Anais got up to go to the kitchen.

"Sounds good to me, kitten," her father said.

"Bring some in to all of us. I think coffee is a good idea. Make it strong, dear," her mother said.

"Are you planning to stay awake all night?" Anais mused. Her mother did not answer her. She looked pensive, as if she had not heard the question that was asked with a raised eyebrow.

Anais was putting water into the pot at the kitchen sink, which sat under a window overlooking a sweep of the grounds. Suddenly, through the brush, Anais saw a shadow move. She quickly turned out the light and went back to the window to see if she could get a better look at whatever it was that was out there. She strained to see through the curtain of snow that was still falling heavily. Once in a while a wind would blow away the icy flakes and for a moment there would be a clearing. There it was again. It could be a deer, she thought; they often came near the house when it snowed. Anais drew up sharply. It was a man, crouching. She leaned against the sink for a moment, her mind racing with thoughts of who it might be. Her eyes raised to the ceiling with a sudden thought of Andy. She raced up the back stairs and ran with the speed of a woman gone mad with fear. When Anais reached Andy's room the door was shut and looked undisturbed. She pushed the door open. The light from the hall cast her shadow on the floor in an angle of yellow light. She peered at the bed, at first unable to discern the shape of the bedding. She moved closer to the bed. Then all the terrors of hell broke loose. She put her hand to her mouth to smother the horrible screams that were flowing from her throat in streams. She could hear her voice calling Andy's name. Anais could see that Andy had been in the bed by the rumpled bedclothing.

Her screams had reached the living room, and as she ran wildly through the front door, her father and E.B. were coming through the living room door as wildly as she was fleeing into the darkness.

"Anais! Anais! Damn it, Anais! Come back here!" her father called after her.

"My God!" Her mother said she saw that Andy was not in his bed.

"For God's sake, get her!" Cora said, running with the rest of a sanguine group of people who suddenly seemed to have gone mad.

The first rush of snow and wind had taken Anais' breath away. She stumbled in the high drifts of snow, which almost reached her knees. She looked wildly around in the direction where she had seen the strange man. There was nothing except the rustling of the snow among the bushes and the rush of the rising wind.

"Andy! Andy!" she called, sobbing into the cold wind that carried her cries away through the night. She had become numb with cold and fear and she could not move any farther. She stood blinded by the snow, her hair whipping across her eyes. In an instant, she saw a yellow flash of light and the sudden cracking sound of rifle fire; off in the distance there was a return of fire. Then a tall figure in a duffle coat and navy woolen watch cap came up behind her. She turned swiftly upon the man, who, without a word, clipped her on the chin and knocked her cold, and she floated into darkness without pain.

When Anais opened her eyes again, she saw her mother and Aunt Cora bending over her with worried expressions. She was lying on the sofa in front of the fire. She put her hand to her head, which throbbed fiercely. She turned her head toward the corner of the room, where something seemed to be going on. She tried to bring her eyes into focus as she stared at the familiar figure standing there. She raised herself up and said, "Arthur?" Then what had gone on before came back to her and she held her hands to her head and said, "Oh, God, they've taken Andy." She began to sob uncontrollably again.

Her mother knelt down beside her quickly and said, "It's all right, darling. Andy is safe."

Anais looked at her mother through red eyes and asked, "Mother, what is going on here?"

"Lie back, Anais, and rest. You're probably going to catch your death of cold," her mother said gently pushing her down again.

Anais looked toward Arthur and wondered why he stood glowering at her with a glacial stare. As her gaze lingered on him she saw that he was wearing strange-looking clothes, clothes that looked like military garb. No one spoke. They all seemed to be shouting at each other in a silence not unlike that of a cat waiting to strike. Her father and E.B. stood in opposite corners watching Arthur. Anais sat up again. The two men from the sheriff's office stood beside Arthur and two other men. They too were dressed in clothes that would be suitable for strenuous activity. As her eyes searched over the group of men, she saw that they both held guns in their hands. She peered wide-eyed at her mother and Aunt Cora. Then she saw the tall man in the duffle coat; he still wore his navy woolen watch cap and held a rifle in his hand.

"What is going on?"

Her mother looked at her husband.

"Remember I asked you about the bonds that E.B. had given Julia?" her father said. "When you didn't know anything about it, I investigated and uncovered a plot that I could never have dreamed in my wildest imagination, and the shocker was that Arthur was one of its principal leaders." Her father looked at Arthur and shook his head sadly. "I'll never understand how you could have done it," he continued.

"I called E.B. and he contacted some friends in Washington. Arthur was always on business trips down in Paraguay; I never could understand what the business was." He left the two men he was standing with and sat down in a chair near his daughter.

"There's a powerful Nazi conclave working out of Paraguay. Some of them escaped prosecution after the war by fleeing there, and some of them are the biggest missing war criminals that were in Hitler's inner circle. And they still hold the dream of coming back to power. They have a lot of help from some very powerful and rich Americans. Then again, just some misguided and very ambitious Americans who dream of power and its glories, and would do anything for it—like kidnap your own son and hold him for ransom. That right, Arthur?"

Anais stood up and looked with horror upon this man whom her loving sister had married.

"How could you! How could you!" were the only words that she could choke out before she flung herself at Arthur, who quickly raised his hand to strike her, but with lightning speed E.B. stepped in and swooped her back. A harnessed rage burned behind his steel-blue eyes as he calmly said, "I wouldn't do that, Arthur."

"No harm would have come to the boy. You know that," Arthur said in reflection.

"How do I know that? Your good sense seems to have been drowned in your ego. So do you think that I can honestly say that you would not have harmed him if it had suited your purpose?" Anais shot back at him.

"Why didn't someone tell me?" Anais looked upon her family with a dumbfounded, quizzical expression that was beginning to border on hysteria.

"Sit down, Anais," her father ordered. "E.B. and I are the protectors of this family. We didn't want any emotions involved. Look at you. The minute you found out, you wanted to tear him apart. And I'll tell you, as long as Andy is safe, I don't give a tinker's damn about Arthur." He smiled at the men holding the guns. "But I imagine that these gentlemen do."

"Anais, I walked in on your father while he was talking to E.B., and I overheard what he was saying about the plot of these people to kidnap Andy. Otherwise I wouldn't have known either, and, of course, if I knew, Cora had to know. Just thank God it's all over now." Her mother heaved a sigh of relief that sent a shudder through her body.

The man in the duffle coat looked at his watch again and spoke to the two other men so softly that his words were inaudible to the rest of the people in the room. Arthur shifted his stance and looked dangerous. Anais' eyes moved toward him. She never knew that she could feel so much hatred; her yellow eyes were filled with malevolence as she stared at him.

"How could you have done this to Julia?" she asked, with bitterness trembling in her voice.

Arthur squirmed a bit under her cold gaze and felt a compulsion to reason with her.

"Julia was a beautiful woman. I only wish she had had more imagination. We could have done things together."

He emphasized "things" and shrugged his shoulders. "Instead, she was a bit stupid about 'things.'"

"The pity is that you stayed so long with a woman whose intellectual capacity did not measure up to your ideals!" Anais shot back at him.

Arthur gave her a twisted smile and said, "Money, money, my dear, Anais. Who has more money than the LaPrells?"

Anais turned away from Arthur with a look of revulsion to stand for a moment in front of the fire, whose peace seemed not in the least bit disturbed by the violence in the room. Cora walked over and stood beside her. The room held a sense of waiting—for what, it was hard to discern, as each floated in and out of his own thoughts.

"We'll be leaving soon," one of the agents, who was holding a .38 revolver, said. "As soon as some more of our men get here with transportation." He waved his gun at Arthur and his two companions and said, "We may as well all sit. . . ." His words were cut off in an explosion of cold air and shattering windowpanes as five men dove through the broken window frame. They carried small submachine guns and pointed them menacingly at the astonished group of people in the room. The drapes blew wildly from the driving snow and wind.

"Drop your guns!" one of the intruders ordered the agents. One of his men swept down quickly and picked the guns up as they were dropped by the agents. He gave the two .38s to each of the men, who seconds ago had been prisoners, and a machine gun to Arthur.

While still in the agony of confusion of being captives,

the group stood helpless, the agents with their hands held above their heads.

They were startled when another figure emerged through the broken window. He dusted the snow from his army fatigues and removed the woolen cap that he wore pulled low over his face. He smiled and said, "Anais, darling. Good evening, Misters and Missus LaPrells."

Anais sat abruptly in the wing chair. If the chair had not been there she would have fallen on the floor.

"Elliott!" She could hardly speak his name from lack of breath.

"Yes, dear?" he answered with a shameless arrogance.

"Elliott, why? Why? You have everything!"

He swaggered over to her chair and leaned over her. Grasping the arms of the chair, he said, "I'm afraid, my dear, that I don't have the time for a long explanation, but let's say, in brief, that my grandfather had all the fun in accumulating a vast family fortune. So . . . I needed something to do." He looked at her with mocking eyes and smiled. "Something interesting; working as a brainless exec just didn't cut it, my love." He stood up and looked down at Anais and asked, "Coming with me, darling?"

She turned her head into the corner of the chair and would not look at him again.

"Let's get going," one of the men said, and in one quick move Arthur reached out and grabbed a startled Cora.

"Throw your coat over here," he said to the agent in the duffle coat. The man removed his coat and flung it to Arthur.

"Here, put this on," he said to Cora. "We don't want

you catching cold, do we?" he said, helping Cora on with the coat.

E.B. had risen from his chair, purple with rage, and had started to move in Arthur's direction, when Arthur raised the muzzle of the gun to Cora's head.

"Stay where you are, E.B. Just remember I never did like any of you very much," Arthur sneered.

Cora twisted her head so that she could see Arthur and said, "It has been a case of award-winning performances, my dear Arthur. You see, the feelings have always been mutual."

"Now we know," he said sarcastically. "Come along now." He turned to the paralyzed group that stood by watching him helplessly.

"In fifteen minutes," he said checking his watch, "come to the end of the drive and pick Cora up. She won't be harmed unless you try some heroics. My advice is, don't." Arthur motioned to the others of his command with a jerk of his head toward the door. "Let's move."

"Don't forget, give us fifteen minutes." Arthur nodded to them and left, pushing Cora ahead of him.

"This is outrageous," E.B. said.

The agent who had been wearing the duffle coat checked his watch and said, "It's exactly one A.M.; we'll wait until one-fifteen and pick Mrs. LaPrell up."

E.B. paced the floor like a pent-up tiger.

Anais went to her uncle and put her arms around him.

"She will be all right, Uncle E.B." She turned to the agents and cried out helplessly, "Can't you do something? They're getting away."

"We'll do as they say, Miss LaPrell. Wait," the agent said, glancing hurriedly in agitation at his watch again. He clasped his hand tightly over the face of the watch and went to the broken window to look out. The other two agents went to peer out into the icy night with him. The cold wind blew into their faces, stinging them with hard pellets of snow.

"Can you see anything?" one of the men asked.

"No," was the somber reply. "I didn't expect him to do anything like this."

"Damn!" was the reply from the third agent.

They checked their watches simultaneously and one of them said, "Let's move out."

They dashed from the house into the station wagon that was still parked in front of the door. The five men got into the car without saying a word to the women, who ran behind them and were left standing in the cold on the doorstep.

The snow tires dug into the snow with a spinning whine and the car took off. Anais and her mother watched the headlights darting against the darkness.

"Come back into the house, Anais. They'll be back soon," her mother said, with a dreadful fear in her chest.

In the car, E.B. swore and said, "If she even breaks a fingernail, I'll kill Elliott and Arthur, and, by God, that's a promise."

The headlights danced erratically against the snow as the car sped along the road. It suddenly came to a skidding halt as the glare of the light beams caught the figure of Cora standing in the middle of the road. It was quite evident that Cora was all right as she shaded her eyes from the glare of the headlights and called, with mock taunting, to the men who were rushing to her: "What took you so long?"

E.B. rushed to his wife with loving arms, and, hugging and kissing her profusely, he demanded to know if she was all right.

"I'm all right," she stated, none the worse for wear. "Just cold." And she was rushed into the waiting car.

in your normal fashion, Arthur's suspicions would not be aroused. We didn't know about Elliott."

"Stupid," Anais interjected with a slight sneer. Cora and her mother failed to comment on her observation.

"Tillie was only told this evening when we went to Adelaide's. That was the time the agents wanted Andy moved out of the house, and, of course, someone that he trusted would have had to go with him, and Tillie is family." Anais' mother clasped her hands together when a surge of memory of the ordeal swept over her, and she stopped speaking for a moment. She found her voice again and continued.

"When I told Tillie, she was ready to go after Arthur herself, which is another reason your father kept it from both of you, but in the end she was needed. They had someone who is an undercover or double agent." She stopped again, then said, "I still find all of this hard to believe. Well, he works for both sides, or they think that he is a part of their organization; he was in on the plan and notified Washington. That was about the time your father discovered that Arthur was floating those bonds that E.B. had given Julia as a wedding present."

"But why, Mother?" Anais asked in bewilderment.

Cora, who was sipping brandy, still trying to throw off the chill that had seeped through her body to the very marrow of her bones, spoke taking a sip of warming brandy and looked at Anais with a steady gaze. "My dear Anais, because Andy must be one of the richest persons alive."

Anais looked at Cora and said, "You mean they were going to kidnap him for the money that he would eventually come into?"

CHAPTER 10

When they arrived back at the house, Cora was surrounded by her concerned family.

"Come into the library, Cora, I don't know who's going to have a worse case of pneumonia—you or Anais," Anais' mother said.

The women went into the library while the men went in search of something to board the broken window up to stop the blowing in of snow that was beginning to pile up along the base of the window.

In the library a cheerful fire burned with crackling logs and dancing flames.

"My God, where is Tillie?" Anais asked. She started out the door when her mother called her back.

"Tillie's fine. She's with Andy," her mother told her.

"Will someone please tell me where my nephew is and how this has all come about? I seem to be the only one that has been in the dark."

Anais was becoming more than a little annoyed as she dropped her graceful but weary body into the wing chair in front of the fire.

"Now that everyone is safe, I think that we can take time and discuss this. You must admit that at the time only Andy's safety mattered, and there was no point in both of us falling apart. As long as you seemed to be going along

"That's right. E.B. and I have only you; you are an only child, and Andy is Julia's heir. Whatever money there is goes to two people and eventually to one. So far. They wanted a lot of money. They could have gotten it, too." Cora's gaze turned to the flickering flames and she said thoughtfully, "No one needs that much money. I think we should speak to the men and set up a working foundation to disburse some of this money."

"I believe you're right, Cora," Anais' mother agreed.

"I think it's a very good idea. I would like to take some part in helping to set it up," Anais said.

"Good idea, Anais," Cora said.

"I think I'll call Adelaide," Anais said, "and see how Andy is."

"Wait until morning. It's two A.M., for heaven's sake, Anais."

"You're right. I'd forgotten."

"Not that it has its bearing on anything, but, Anais, I never could stand that man you were engaged to," Cora said. "Too much of a snob. In the true sense of the dictionary definition."

Anais looked thoughtfully into the fire, closing her mother and Cora out for the moment. She traveled back to the beginning of her romance with Elliott. Then, Anais noticed the steady gaze of Cora over the rim of her brandy glass.

"Honey, I want you to know that in this family we married out of love for each other, and not out of fear of hurting the family's feelings because we changed our minds. A thrill goes through my whole body when I see your uncle coming toward me, and we've been married a long time. I don't know if you've ever noticed, but sometimes at the dinner table, when there have been no fewer than twenty people, I've seen your father catch your mother's eye and wink at her; that's letting her know that she is still the most important thing in his life, and he's glad that she is there. Anything less in a marriage is a waste of life." Cora took another sip of brandy and Anais wiped away a tear. "This brandy is good. It warms the body and loosens the tongue. I might just get drunk. I'm cold and I have a lot to say."

This brought a smile to Anais' face and to her mother's, who had been watching her daughter with deep concern.

Anais' father and E.B. came through the door. Their presence filled the room like two big bulls, well in command of the situation.

"We've got that window boarded up. It should keep the snow out until we can get Jemerson here tomorrow," her father announced.

"Where are the agents?" Anais asked.

"Gone," E.B. said.

"Do you think that they will catch up with them?" Anais asked, fear again rising in her. "If they don't, Andy will still be in danger and it's going to be the same thing all over again. Oh, my God." Anais clamped her hand over her mouth for fear of screaming.

Her father went to her and put his arm around her shoulders. "I promise you, honey, there's no longer any danger to Andy. We can all go to bed now and have a good night's sleep—what's left of it anyway," he said.

Cora stretched her still good long legs and said, "E.B., I think you should carry me upstairs."

"If you say so," E.B. replied and swept a giggling Cora up in his big arms and carried her out of the room.

"Are my two girls ready?" Anais' father asked, reaching out to her mother. She placed her small hand in his and he clamped his strong fingers around hers. Anais got up and he put his arm around her waist and they went upstairs together. Their steps were slow. It had been a long day and night.

CHAPTER 11

A silver-blue dawn rose over a still, snow-covered land that masked the wounds of the harrowing night that had just passed. Nothing seemed touched by man, and a silence hummed through the trees, where songless sparrows nestled like little round gray balls on the branches.

Anais watched the sky brightening as she lay with the covers pulled up to her chin. It seemed that of late she had watched many daybreaks, and as life will have it, most who watch the birth of a new day do it with a heavy heart.

The room was warm from the central heating. The fire in the fireplace was now only a few glowing embers in the ash.

Anais got up and looked out of the window. The snow had stopped and it looked like everyone's dream of a white Christmas. She dressed and went down to the kitchen. She was beginning to feel uneasy about Andy and was anxious to get to him.

Helga was already in the kitchen, and as usual, the kitchen smelled of perking coffee and something good baking.

"Good morning, Helga," Anais said with a touch of weariness.

"Ah, sit down, Miss Anais, and have some coffee. After

last night I suppose I should offer you a good strong brandy, but I guess coffee will do," Helga said, wiping her hands on her apron. She continued chatting. "You know, when I saw von Stressmann the week he spent up here with Mr. Elliott and Mr. Arthur"—Anais flinched at the mention of Elliott and Arthur's names, but Helga took no notice—"I knew"—and she stressed the words with a wagging of her finger—"I knew that I had seen him somewhere before." She put her finger to her temple, "But where kept escaping me. Many times I almost had it, then, just like that"—Helga snapped her fingers—"it was gone before I got it. And for the longest time it bothered me. And then those two gentlemen came up after you left and showed me a photograph, much younger, but it was him all right. Dr. Emil Streicher, the butcher." Helga shook her head sadly. "He performed surgical atrocities in all of the concentration camps that no human being could believe. *Mein Gott*," Helga said, lapsing into her native German.

Anais slumped back in her chair and said, "I don't understand anything, Helga. I found this man charming and I was two seconds from inviting him to dinner to talk about the beauty of Rome." She drew in a deep breath and it emitted as a sigh.

Helga took a seat. She was now engrossed in their conversation.

"Do you know what it is, Miss Anais? Now you take the riffraff that hang around the streets. We don't want to go near them. They look squalid, so we give them a wide berth, but"—Helga wagged her finger again—"wear a fine suit and look good in a tuxedo and you can take the world to hell and back." Helga drew back and said, "Forgive me, Miss Anais, I speak too much."

"I agree with you, Helga. I would never dream of asking some poor soul in Times Square to dinner, but had I not been interrupted I would have asked a distinguished-looking mass murderer, with very good manners and looking for a second chance to complete what he had started, to dine with me. I feel like such a fool, Helga, such a fool."

There was a noise at the front door and in moments Anais' father and E.B. entered the kitchen. They were wearing the bright plaid hunting jackets that they had worn on the day of Anais' arrival, which seemed another life ago.

"What about picking up that grandson of mine? The roads are clear now and we can have breakfast with Tillie and Andy."

"That sounds like a good idea to me," Anais said, leaving the kitchen to get her things.

"Your mother and Cora are ready," her father called to her.

Anais had thought that she was the only one up, but it seemed that she had not watched the breaking of day alone.

Everyone was silently jittery, as the station wagon squished along the road over the melting snow. Each one in his own mind was certain that the boy was safe, but until their eyes beheld Andy, their nerves would remain raw.

Anais spoke suddenly to her father, who was at the wheel of the car.

"Daddy, you've passed Adelaide's driveway."

"I know, honey. Andy's not at Adelaide's."

"He's not? Where is he?" She was now at a loss for words. As she groped for words, the car turned onto a small dirt road that climbed upward. Anais looked about in bewilderment.

"Why, this is the Merriwether place."

"Yeah," her father answered. "We thought it best to have Andy at a place they would not have thought about. Adelaide and Jim's place would have been their first thought if Andy had not been home."

"Yes, of course," Anais said in a siege of confusion.

"It was real nice of that young feller to come up and open his house for us."

Anais was now watching the edges of white road and barely listening to her father.

"Jim drove all the way back to New York to get him; we didn't want to say anything over the phone."

"Lucky he bought that house," her father said, shaking his head at their good fortune.

The Merriwether house sat on a hill overlooking the fall of the land. It was a beautiful pre-Revolutionary War house, with evergreen trees dotting the land, and one large holly tree with bright-red berries gave color to the quiet white morning.

They stamped the snow from their boots and rang the doorbell. Footsteps were heard coming down the entrance hall and Anais' heart was hammering in her chest as she strove to master calmness. But when the door opened, it was Tillie who stood there and not Gathen. Tillie took Anais in her arms and they both started to cry.

"Come on in," Tillie said. "No need to stand out here and freeze to death." She wiped her eyes with the corner of an apron that she had found in the pantry.

The house was filled with beautiful early-American furniture. Wall niches displayed porcelain plates, Chinese and Staffordshire, a collection that looked rare and well thought out. The house had been left exactly as it had been when Mrs. Merriwether had been alive. The heirs had obviously had no interest in the past nor in the history of the house, other than dividing the cash from the sale of it.

"Come on, Andy's in the living room with Mr. Bentley," Tillie said, leading the way.

"Now would be the moment," Anais thought.

Tillie opened a double door and Anais saw a man and a little boy framed by a large window, sitting at a grand piano, and the little boy was picking out the classic "Chopsticks." The boy had one leg tucked under him, while the other dangled down from the piano bench in rhythm to the tune. The man held the forefingers of the child, and they were completely engrossed in their music. The small group stood for a moment in the doorway watching them, until Gathen looked up.

"How can I ever thank you, Gathen?" Anais said from the doorway.

"I don't think there's any reason to try." He smiled at her.

"I see you two know each other," her father said.

"Yes," was Anais' reply.

"Come here, young man, and let Grandpa have a look at you," her father called to Andy, who immediately got up from the piano and ran to his grandfather and gave him a big hug, as always, but if Andy had been older, he would have sensed that it was not as always, as his grandfather closed his eyes in a moment of thanks and patted his grandson's back.

"Well, I've made breakfast," Tillie announced, relieving the tension of agonizing joy.

"I'm for that," E.B. said, following Tillie.

Anais walked with Gathen to the kitchen. "The house is lovely."

"I'm glad you like it. You must come sometime and see it."

"I'd love to," she said as they entered the large country kitchen where a roaring fire burned brightly in a huge fireplace that the colonists had once used to cook their meals. The heavy iron rod was still in place and held an iron kettle. Pewter plates lined the mantelpiece with four pewter candlesticks interspersed between them.

The table was set with earthenware breakfast dishes, with country butter and hot rolls steaming on the table. Tillie put hot sausages and scrambled eggs on the plates.

"Come on, Tillie, sit down. We can serve ourselves," Anais' father said. "It's a good morning," he said, smiling broadly.

Tillie sat down next to Anais. "It was a hard night," she said softly to Anais.

"Tillie slept in my room last night," Andy announced happily.

"That was fun, I bet," Anais said, watching her nephew still with some apprehension; though the morning seemed serene and warm, the thought never left her mind that the men who had planned this abominable deed had escaped, and at this moment were God knows where. Through the haze of her thoughts, she heard her father's voice saying to Gathen, "Do you have any plans for Christmas?" He looked hopefully that Gathen would not, but Gathen had to disappoint him, and he said regretfully, "Adelaide and Jim have asked me to Christmas dinner."

"Oh, that's too bad. But you will come some other time?" her father said.

"Yes, thank you, sir." Gathen smiled.

Gathen would glance discreetly every once in a while in Anais' direction under the false notion that no one saw his secret glances, but they had not gone unnoticed either by Anais' mother or by her aunt, and Tillie already knew, and it was not from anything that had been said to her.

After breakfast they sat around the kitchen table talking as they watched the bright flames dance up the chimney.

Anais said, "I think we had better help Gathen get the kitchen cleaned up." They all pitched in and had the kitchen spotless with all the dishes put into the dishwasher. With this done, they prepared to leave. At the door, Anais' father took Gathen's hand and said, "Son, if you ever need anything, and I mean anything, nothing will ever be too big. Just let me know." He patted Gathen on the shoulder and they took their leave.

Adelaide's car was standing in the driveway when they arrived back at the house. She sat in the library sipping coffee. She looked around when she heard Anais enter the room.

"Oh, my dear," she said, hurrying to embrace Anais. "What a hellish ordeal this has been."

Anais returned her embrace and closed her weary eyes for a moment. "I'm afraid it's not over yet." She sat down in the wing chair before the fire, and Adelaide returned to her seat on the sofa.

"Adelaide, the scandal. Can you even begin to imagine the horror when the press gets hold of this? And the worst part is, they're still free." She covered her eyes for a moment and continued. "It's Andy that I'm thinking of. I think I'll take him down to Mayhill, the press is barely aware of Mother's home, and we can hide for a while in the hills of Virginia. I hope." She stopped talking and began to sort out her thoughts while Adelaide watched sympathetically with pain spilling from her eyes.

"Do that. He mustn't be exposed to this, Anais. There might be serious psychological damage. So take him away in a few days, as soon as Christmas is over. Jim will be away on business and I will come down and stay for a few days. It's going to be all right, it's just going to take a bit of careful thinking," she said. Silence filled the room for a few moments before Adelaide broke it by saying, "I've invited Gathen over tonight for a light supper. You wouldn't care to come, I suppose?" Adelaide asked without much hope of Anais accepting.

"I think not, Adelaide. Thanks anyway." She looked at Adelaide soberly and said, "I almost wish that they wouldn't catch them. Let them go back to Paraguay and hide for the rest of their lives."

Adelaide looked at Anais, equally as sober, and said, "But they are very dangerous men."

"Oh, anything to save Andy from what will happen when they do catch up with them."

"I know, dear." Adelaide patted her hand.

Anais looked down at her hands and said, "It was very kind of Gathen to come up and take Andy to his house."

"Well, I'm sure you know how he felt about that. I believe he stayed up all night keeping watch with Jim."

"We are blessed with good friends." Anais spoke with deep sincerity.

"Aren't we all. I really must go now and help Jim pick up the tree. It always falls over several times before we finally get it to stand up, knocking over everything in its way." Adelaide spread her hands out and laughed. "See you." And she left.

Christmas day dawned like a Grandma Moses painting. Smoke curled from chimneys into a gray sky, as bright Christmas lights of red, green, blue, and yellow twinkled on green fir trees that were covered with snow.

The LaPrell house seemed no different on this Christmas morning than any other happy house, and only the adult members of the family knew that this Christmas was indeed different.

Anais saw Andy's head poke around her door, and he said in a loud whisper, "Anais, is it time to go down?"

Anais looked at the clock beside her bed: it read 5 A.M. exactly. She raised herself up on her elbows and reluctantly said, "I suppose so."

"Good. I'll get Grandma and Grandpa, and Uncle E.B. and Aunt Cora." Andy was gone in a rush of wind to awaken the rest of the household and to announce that it was Christmas.

The family assembled in the living room in a variety of dressing gowns. The gifts were many and expensive: F. A. O. Schwarz had abounded by the LaPrell family. There were large boxes and small boxes with distinguished names, such as Saks Fifth Avenue, Neiman-Marcus, Cartier, and Tiffany. Anais picked up a slender Cartier box, the tag said to "Anais, with love, Elliott." Anais was sickened by the gift and she thought, "So he was going to play it to the very end." She handed the box to her mother saying, "Give this to charity, whatever it is." She left the room so that Andy would not sense any emotional change.

After breakfast Andy went back to his toys and Anais thought this a good time to take Adelaide and Jim's presents to them while the rest of the family had a few quiet moments.

Adelaide's tree was now standing in its full glory, with tiny white lights, silver balls, and silver garlands draped around its thick needles. This was a grown-up Christmas tree, very elegant and uniform, not the rainbow of lights and balls on their tree at home, which was still decorated with a child in mind.

"Merry Christmas, darling," Adelaide called to Anais from under the tree. "I saw your car and I'm pulling your presents from under the tree." She got up, pulling some of the silver tinsel with her.

"Here you are, darling. I think you're going to like it."

"Here's yours, for you and Jim," Anais said, opening her gift.

"Why it's lovely, Adelaide. Thank you so much." Anais held up a small delicate gold mesh evening purse.

"I saw you admire it that day in Rome, and I went right back the next day and bought it. Shopping in September beats the December rush." Adelaide smiled, pleased that Anais liked her present.

"Do you know I went back the next day to get it, and the saleswoman told me that it had been sold?" Anais was still admiring her purse when Adelaide unwrapped her present.

"Oh! I can't believe it," Adelaide cried. "Look, Jim, it's a Tao-chi ink and watercolor. Oh! Anais, how lovely." Adelaide kissed Anais. "Oh, I have something else for you. It's not from us." Adelaide went under the tree again and came up with a flat, square, beautifully wrapped package. "Here you are, darling."

"Oh," Anais said as she opened the gift. "Oh, my, how beautiful."

It was Gathen's first album and it bore a lovely photograph of him sitting at the piano.

Anais held the album to her chest for a moment. Adelaide turned to the door as Gathen came in.

"I didn't think you would mind." Gathen grinned at her. "Merry Christmas, Anais."

"Merry Christmas, Gathen," she said. "I want to thank you again for coming up to take Andy. You know, you have endeared yourself for life to my father. He will try to push everything on you; just be very firm with him and he will soon understand your way. But he is so grateful and so am I."

"Well, it's over now. Let's put it in the past. How did Santa Claus treat Andy?" Gathen asked, changing the subject.

"Much too well, I'm afraid, and he's enjoying every moment of it."

When Anais returned home, an early Christmas dinner was being readied. Neighbors were dropping in to wish the joys of the season and to have some of the fluffy, potent eggnog that Helga had prepared. The house not only looked like Christmas, but it smelled of Christmas. The roasting turkey and the aroma of baking pies filled the rooms, and the most pungent fragrance was that of the Christmas tree. When Anais walked into the house, it was the first time that she had felt the spirit of Christmas, and she kept hidden from herself that it was because she had seen Gathen.

Christmas dinner drew to a close with the thankful prayer that this particular Christmas be a happy one and the usual groans after a Christmas dinner of being overstuffed.

Dusk moved across the quiet Connecticut countryside, and the family settled into a quiet close of another Christmas. They were quietly talking when the phone rang. Helga came to the door and said, "You're wanted on the telephone, Mr. LaPrell."

"I'll take it in here." He went to a small table sitting in the corner of the room. When he heard the voice on the other end of the wire, he immediately regretted his decision.

"Yeah, how goes it?" he asked discreetly, but all eyes and ears had turned to him with quizzical looks.

"I see." He was quiet while the voice on the other end said, "The plane is down in the Andes." He paused for a moment, then continued, after mulling over his thoughts. "We brought the plane down over the highest range. Rescuers cannot reach it, and snow is covering the wreckage. There are no survivors." Mr. LaPrell flinched at these words, and all he could say, so that the other party on the other end of the wire could know that he was still on the phone, was, "I see."

"We thought it best this way, letting them make their escape. You wouldn't have wanted any shooting at your home. The memory would always be with you and every living soul would have wanted to know why. This way it's just a terrible family tragedy. A little boy has lost his father in a plane crash, and you can mourn him properly, and our job is finished. We still have the senator, but he is now small potatoes." The voice paused again, then said, "They had partially paid for enough arms to supply a good-sized army." His voice trailed off again, then he said, "It was better this way. I am sorry, sir."

The calm, matter-of-fact voice had stunned Anais' father and he could barely get the words "Thank you" out.

"Good-bye, sir," the voice said, and Mr. LaPrell knew that he would never hear that calm, deadly voice again.

He returned to the small group, who eyed him with a foreboding expectation. He sat down heavily on the sofa. He certainly held no affection for Elliott or Arthur, but this threw him off balance and he tried to make his recovery as quickly as he possibly could, which was not easy.

Mr. LaPrell waved a hand toward the door and said, "Will someone see that Andy is with Helga?"

Anais hurried up from her chair and said, "I will, Daddy." She did not take her eyes off of her father, which were filled with the fear of the unknown, as she left the room. She soon returned to the room and said, "Andy's with Karl. What is it, Daddy?"

"Sit down, Anais." Her father prepared himself as to what he would tell them and what he would not. Later on he would fill E.B. in on every detail. But he would not tell the women that the plane had been deliberately sent down. They sat quietly as he replayed the telephone conversation.

Anais sat as taut as a wire, her hands clasped so tightly in her lap that the blood had stopped flowing through them.

"We're going back to the city tomorrow when we get the official news. We'll do our mourning and hope to hell that the press lets it go without any investigative reporting," her father said with a certain amount of contempt in his voice, "but just in case they don't buy it, Anais, you're to take Andy somewhere else that's safe to stay until we're sure this thing has blown over."

"Yes, I've already thought of that," Anais said. "We will stay at Gathen's house."

"Well, that's that," he stated. "I think it's over."

"Dear God, I hope so," her mother said.

E.B. and Cora were silent, which was odd for both of them. E.B. finally spoke and his voice was subdued. "We're going to go on with our lives, just as we have always lived." He heaved a deep sigh. "Not really, I suppose."

"I think I'll turn in," Anais' father said. "You coming, hon?" he asked his wife.

"Yes, I think we should all go to bed and try to rest," she replied.

Timothy drove up to Connecticut to take the family back to New York. Anais sat in the corner of the car watching the snow-covered roadside passing in a blur as the car sped along the parkway. Her mother sat between her and Cora; her father and E.B. sat on the jump seats facing them. Andy and Tillie sat in front with Timothy. There was very little said on the trip back to the city. They each took turns breathing in deep breaths of air, like actors awaiting their turn to go onstage.

The long black Continental limousine pulled up in front of the Park Avenue residence of the LaPrells. Mr. LaPrell pushed the button and rolled down the glass that separated them from the front seat and said to Tillie, "You and Andy get out first. Take him right in, Tillie."

"Yes," was Tillie's understanding reply.

Timothy got out and opened the front door first, acting as a shield for Andy and Tillie. The doorman held the door wide for them as he waited to close it immediately after they entered. Andy looked about the crowd of reporters with wide eyes of incomprehension as a few of them took pictures of him. Tillie had him inside the door and on the elevator in a matter of seconds.

Timothy opened the back door of the car. There was a collective intake of air. The curtain was up and the show was on, as they each stepped from the car. Anais' father and E.B. shielded the women from the reporters, and her father said, "Gentlemen, this is a terrible tragedy." As he spoke these words, he was careful not to use the word "grief." Somehow he could carry his playacting just so far. "You understand that the family must handle this the best way that we can. Soon, when we are able to, we will release a press statement." He waved his hand to the reporters and followed his family into the apartment building. The reporters drifted off in different directions with a neither-here-nor-there report. Arthur's death was not that important as far as they were concerned. He had never done anything that was particularly outstanding, except to marry into one of the richest families in the country. If they had known to what extent Arthur had gone not to have that as his epitaph, they would have had the story of the decade.

There was a simple memorial service at a church on Park Avenue. A small group of family friends gathered at the service. A minister spoke a few kind words about Arthur. They were words that were made up out of respect to the family, because the minister had not known Arthur.

After the services, the family stood on a receiving line at the entrance of the church to receive the condolences of friends. Anais was surprised to see Gathen waiting on the steps of the church. He did not make any effort to speak to Anais or to her family, but he regarded her with compassion from his distance on the steps. When the last person came to express his sympathy, Anais again glanced toward the steps, but Gathen was no longer there.

A solitary group that could not speak against the blustering winds that blew across Flushing Bay made their way to a Lear jet that sat in a far corner of the airfield against a background of dingy gray snow that had been soiled by the exhaust of jet fuel. The wings of the plane bobbed up and down, as if straining to get on with the job it had been created for.

The lonely group boarded the plane and were greeted by the captain, who helped Cora and E.B. take off their coats; he then took Andy with him up to the cockpit so that the LaPrells could talk in private.

The weary group stood silently, seemingly not knowing what to say next, around a conference table that E.B. used to hold meetings with his executives while en route from one office to another.

"It was good of Gathen to offer us his house. So far hardly anyone knows that he has bought the old Merriwether house and will not connect the families yet," Anais' father said, then added with a sidewise glance at Anais, "I like that young man."

Still standing and shifting from foot to foot, the forlorn group saw a glimmer of light at the dark and ominous tunnel.

"We will soon know whether or not the press has bought Arthur's accidental death or not. We'll just have to wait it out as calmly as possible," Mr. LaPrell said.

"So far so good," Cora said, crossing her fingers.

"Andy just cannot know this," Anais said, with a shake of her head.

"If it happens, Anais, we will deal with it. So there's no

point in worrying about something that might not happen. We'll cross that bridge when we get to it." Mrs. LaPrell spoke firmly.

E.B. put his arms around Anais' shoulders and hugged her to him. "I think it's going to be all right."

Anais gave her uncle a feeble smile. She had always believed in the powers of her father and her uncle, and she half believed that her uncle knew what he was talking about now.

All heads suddenly turned toward the cockpit as they heard one of the plane's engines start up.

"Well, E.B."—Anais' father put his hand out to his brother with love and appreciation—"I guess we had better let you get this thing off the ground."

E.B. grasped his brother's hand tightly, smiled, and said, "This has been one hell of a Christmas."

Anais' mother put her arms around her tall brother-in-law and said, "May we never have another like it."

"I'll drink to that," he replied soberly.

For the first time some of Cora's stamina seemed to falter. When she raised her arms to embrace Anais, tears filled her green eyes and her lips trembled for a second. Through all of this she felt that Anais had been hurt the most. Somehow age not only made you wiser, it buffered pain because you no longer expected life to be perfect. She held her niece tightly.

"If you need E.B. and me, you know that we will be here as fast as this plane can carry us." She held Anais' face in her hand and said, "Take good care, darling."

Cora and E.B. waved good-bye from the door of the plane; an attendant closed the door and Anais and her

family watched the sleek silver jet lumber down the runway, gathering velocity as it rolled along the slushy tarmac. With one last thrust of its powerful engines, it split the blustering winds and was airborne.

Andy waved excitedly as the plane climbed into the air. It dipped one silver wing in farewell before disappearing behind the gray clouds.

Anais looked at the gray clouds and said, "They haven't been gone five minutes and I miss them desperately."

"They'll be back soon. If I know Cora and E.B., they will have some excuse for coming back almost every weekend," her father said.

Tillie opened the door before Anais could get her keys out. Her whole being seemed to be that of controlled jitters.

"Did Mr. and Mrs. LaPrell get off all right?" she asked as the family walked through the doorway.

"Yes, everything went smoothly, although I think I saw some reporters hanging about as we drove up," Mrs. LaPrell said. She dropped her coat on the sofa. "So the sooner you and Anais leave the better. Just in case," she added with a furtive look toward the window.

"Everything is ready," Tillie replied somberly.

"Okay. I'll take a cab downtown and Timothy can drive you to Connecticut," her father said, giving his wife a questioning look.

"If you will get a taxi for me, dear, I'll go home and call Miss Lilis at home and tell her that Andy will be out o school for a while. And Anais has already called t Meadows Day School in Connecticut and Andy can st

after the holidays. It will give him a little time to adjust," she said sadly.

"He'll be all right, honey. He knows quite a few of the kids up there." Her husband's understanding reply brought a hesitant smile to her lips.

"I know. I just wish it were next year this time," she said.

"It'll be over soon," he answered.

Gathen was waiting on the steps when the black limousine pulled up in the driveway. He seemed to have been waiting with the same impatience that had afflicted Tillie back in New York. Anais observed him from the window of the car and thought him very handsome in gray flannel slacks and dark crew-neck sweater with the shirt collar open. She thought, too, that he never seemed to dress warmly enough.

Gathen walked down the steps to the car and opened both the back door and the front door simultaneously and Andy scrambled from the front seat and ran into a snow-drift. Gathen watched him for a moment with a broad grin. He called to Andy, "I'll join you later, sport." He turned his attention to Anais, who was stepping from the car. Their eyes locked for a moment in confusion. He took her hand and helped her from the car, and then Tillie. Tillie gazed up at the house as if seeing it for the first time.

"Go right in where it's warm. I'll help Timothy with the luggage," Gathen said.

When they were settled in, Gathen apologized for not being able to cook, but he had brought Chinese food from the village and some hamburgers for Andy, who he as-

sumed might not have developed a taste for foreign cuisines, which delighted Andy. After lunch, Tillie busied herself with becoming acquainted with a new kitchen. Adelaide called and asked if she could pick Andy up and take him home with her to play with the young son of a houseguest. Anais was at first uncertain about letting Andy out of her sight, but she thought better of it, and decided that she could not keep him locked away from people forever. She asked Timothy to take him and to stay at Adelaide's until it was time for Andy to come back.

"I wish I didn't worry so when Andy goes away, but I do feel better knowing that Timothy's with him." She smiled, with a small feeling of being silly.

"It will take a while before things get back to normal," Gathen said sympathetically.

"Thank you for not thinking me foolish," she said gratefully.

"Come, let me show you the house. You haven't seen it yet."

"Oh! I'd love to. We knew the Merriwethers only as neighbors, so I have never been through the house," Anais said, turning from her vigil of an empty driveway.

"Let's start here in the entrance hall." Gathen pointed to an old spinning wheel that sat near the door. "Look at this. It is never to be taken by any of the owners when they sell the house. It must always stay with the house. It's in the deed."

"Why?" Anais asked.

"It is supposed to bring good fortune to whoever owns the house. The family who built the house felt so blessed with happiness after the arrival of the spinning wheel that they wanted whoever came after them to be blessed with the same love and happiness that had been bestowed upon them, and I guess they thought that it came through the spinning wheel."

A melancholy look passed over Gathen's face. He quickly recovered as he glanced at her. She said softly, "I do hope the same for its new owner."

"We shall see, won't we?" he said coolly and turned toward the beautiful curving cherry stairs that had never been painted and the rich brown wood glowed against the sunny yellow wall leading up to the second floor.

The spacious hall was carpeted with a long oriental rug of cobalt blue with pale orange and pink flowers scattered throughout its rich background. Graceful windows overlooked the driveway. Gathen opened the door to the master bedroom, where a cheery fire burned in the grate. It was a large comfortable room with large windows spanning the wall. Anais observed the room from the doorway. Gathen steered her away to look at the rest of the bedrooms, all of which had logs laid to be lighted.

"I'll show you the rest of downstairs. How do you like it so far?" he asked.

"It's lovely," she replied.

Gathen led Anais to the living room, where a fire blazed in the large stone fireplace. The back of the house where the living room was situated posed a view that could be described as no less than spectacular. From its vantage point, where it stood high on a hill, the house overlooked an icy silver lake which flowed snugly in the shadows of misty rolling hills dotted with lacy dark bare branches that danced over the snow-covered ground in the winter wind.

Anais caught her breath, rushed to the bay window, and knelt on the chintz-covered seat to take in the sweeping view.

"Oh! Gathen, what a magnificent view." She gazed over the fall of the land, then glanced down at the snow-covered stone terrace that lay beneath the window and said, "How marvelous it will be here in the summer."

Gathen smiled distantly, as if his thoughts were elsewhere.

The afternoon passed swiftly. Anais and Gathen chatted before the fire of many things, none of which had any serious note. Andy returned, very pleased with his day: the boy whom he had met at Adelaide's was also attending the Meadows School, and that made him happy to have a new friend. After telling Anais of his swell day, Andy went off to fill Tillie in on his activities.

Gathen sat with Anais for a while longer, although it seemed that any further conversation was lost to the yellow licking flames that glowed brighter as the blue dusk of evening crept through the window and spread across the room.

"I had better leave now and let you get settled." Gathen broke the stillness that, like the dusk, had filled the room. Anais had dreaded this moment when Gathen would leave her.

"Won't you stay for dinner?" she asked, hoping to delay his departure as long as possible.

"No, thank you. I can't this evening." He offered no explanation.

"Then do come whenever you can," Anais said pleasantly, trying to mask her disappointment. She walked with Gathen to the door, her hands clasped tensely before her. She looked up at him and smiled when they reached the door. He bent and kissed her lightly on the cheek.

"Take care," he said.

Anais stood in the fading light and watched Gathen walk away, and an uneasy feeling of emptiness crept over her. She wondered if, after all this, she might have lost Gathen.

The following day Adelaide called and in her usual exuberant voice said, "Good morning, dear. It's really so nice having you up here—just think, not having the rush of New York. We can talk endlessly. But at this moment, I'm calling to ask you to come to a small New Year's Eve party. Just some of the people from around here. Can you come? It will do you good to get out." Adelaide paused for an answer.

"Yes, I'd like to come," Anais replied.

"Oh, I'm glad, darling. Shall I send Jim for you?"

"No, thank you. Timothy is staying with us. He will bring me."

"Fine. See you then." Adelaide was gone and Anais smiled to herself and wondered what had happened to the lazy, easygoing country life. She hung the receiver up and prepared to look for a dress to wear on New Year's Eve. As she went through her clothes, she wondered if Gathen would be there. She had not dared ask Adelaide.

New Year's Eve found Anais filled with anticipation as she dressed for the evening. She did not know whether Gathen would be at the party, but she hoped desperately that he would be and that he would put her mind to rest, that he had not changed in his feelings for her and would be the same warm Gathen that she had known and loved so dearly.

She went downstairs to the living room, where she was greeted with admiration by Tillie, Timothy, and Andy.

"You look pretty, Anais," Andy said.

Anais turned around for them as a model would to show off her dress, which was black silk with a large pink floral print with a blouson back. The skirt tapered off to the hem around her ankles.

"Oh! Anais, you look lovely." Tillie cupped her hands to her beaming face while Timothy, who was not very good at words such as these, just stood grinning his approval.

Andy tugged at Anais' arm. "Tillie said that I can stay up until midnight with her and Timothy and watch the new year come."

"Lovely." Anais kissed Andy and then Tillie. "Happy, happy New Year." She smiled and, not to leave Timothy out, gave him a big kiss on the cheek, which left Timothy blushing like a schoolboy.

Timothy dropped Anais at Adelaide's at ten o'clock. He stood beside the car until she was let in, then drove back to join Andy and Tillie for their little party.

Adelaide's house glowed in the warmth of candlelight. There was not one electric light burning and the night gave birth to the reign of magic. Soft music floated in the pine-scented room, and as Anais entered she was captivated by the phantom of hope that each New Year's brings.

Anais looked about the room, absorbing the spirit of the evening. When her eyes had adjusted to the faint yellow candlelight, she saw the person whom she had been secretly straining to see. Gathen stood in the flickering shadows with two other men, one of whom she recognized as Wells, and a glowing pretty blond woman in an apple-green sequined jacket and long silk crepe dress of the same color. The men were all obviously taken with her beauty and charm, as they laughingly vied for her attention. She seemed to sparkle with delight at their flirtation and her sequined jacket sent spears of light flashing across the room as she moved seductively among them.

Disappointment and jealousy flooded through Anais' body as she watched the merry group, and she toyed with the idea of running from the room, but before she could go any further with the thought, Adelaide came upon her and interrupted any such plans.

"Isn't it lovely to have just a few friends for New Year's Eve," she said to Anais. Twenty was Adelaide's idea of a small gathering.

"Yes," Anais said without much enthusiasm as Adelaide led her into the thick of the party, greeting guests as they moved along slowly to their final destination, Gathen, who was deep in playful conversation.

"Look who's here." Adelaide barged into the midst of their talking.

"Anais!" Wells greeted her with a glad kiss. "So good to see you, hon."

The woman looked around in surprise as she flung her golden hair away from her face and smiled uncertainly at the intrusion. She offered her hand to Anais, who graciously took it.

Gathen smiled down at her and said distantly, "How are you, Anais?" He neither offered his hand nor kissed her on the cheek, as Wells and Miss Lucinda Bridges had done.

Anais excused herself from the group and joined some of the other guests on the far side of the room. She sat listening to conversation that she did not hear. At eleven o'clock she wandered away from the festive bantering, went into the study, where no one else had ventured, and quietly picked up the phone. She heard Tillie's voice come over the wire.

"Tillie, would you ask Timothy to pick me up, please? At the back door."

"Now!" Tillie asked, somewhat bewildered.

"Yes, now," Anais said softly and hung up.

Anais waited in the shadow of the doorway for Timothy to come; she pulled the collar of her fur coat up around her head, clasping the lapels tightly to her chest; her sandaled feet were becoming like chunks of ice. Her hair blew in confusion around her face. She brushed it back from her eyes, where tears had gathered and frozen. She was gripped in a vise of self-pity. She was so numb from the indifference that Gathen had shown her that she felt she could not even die.

The headlights of the car broke the darkness as it turned around the side of the house. Anais dashed into the car before Timothy could alight and open the door for her. He turned to face her in the back seat and asked, "What's the matter, miss?"

"Nothing. I just don't feel very festive tonight," she replied dryly and sank into the corner of the car.

Flurries of snow were beginning to fall as they drove back to Gathen's house in silence except for the squishing of the windshield wipers against the glass.

Tillie was waiting in the entrance hall as Anais suspected she would be.

"What was wrong with the party?" she asked.

"Nothing. I just don't think I'm quite ready for people yet."

"Well, come into the kitchen and have some eggnog," Tillie said, eyeing Anais suspiciously.

Timothy was already in the kitchen when Tillie and Anais entered.

"Where's Andy?" Anais asked.

"Oh, he tried very hard to make it to the new year, miss, but the sandman overpowered him and I took him up to bed," Timothy said humorously. "He's sound asleep, had his eggnog, though." He smiled.

Anais smiled at Andy's failed attempt to greet the incoming year and she thought that being a child had its definite advantages: one slept easily. Anais sat down to the kitchen table in her beautiful party dress. Tillie dipped thick frothy eggnog from the cut-glass bowl, set the cups before Anais and Timothy, and sat down to join them.

"Well, another year has gone by," she said philosophically.

"So it has," Anais said, gazing sadly into the roaring fire.

Suddenly the clock started to chime and in the distant night they could hear the sounds of noisemakers and horns greeting the first minute of the new year.

"Happy New Year, honey," Tillie said leaning over to

embrace Anais. Anais stretched both her hands over the table and grasped Timothy's.

"Happy New Year, miss," Timothy said grinning.

"It's going to be a good year," Tillie said, holding her glass up in a salute.

Anais rose from her chair and said, "Now that we have greeted the new year, I think I shall go to bed." Anais knew that she would not share the same easy sleep tonight as Andy, but she had to be alone with her tormented thoughts.

"Oh, Adelaide telephoned," Tillie called to Anais. "She couldn't imagine what had happened to you. I told her that Timothy was bringing you home. She'll call you tomorrow." Anais made no reply as she left the room, and Tillie said thoughtfully to Timothy, "I'll be glad when she is settled." She raised her glass. "Happy New Year, Tim."

CHAPTER 12

Despite Tillie's less than enthusiastic stay in Connecticut, time did not seem endless. Andy was enrolled at the Meadows Day School and he kept busy with new friends, whose families had been friends of the LaPrells for many years.

Anais kept abreast of the newspapers. She had all of the New York papers sent up to her, just in case there was the smallest indication in the society columns or political pieces, whose items were held a shade above the out-and-out gossip columnists. It all boiled down to the same thing.

In her diligent scanning of the newspapers, she did read in one of the gossip columns that Gathen had been on a four-month concert tour of Europe, and that lately he had been seen quite often in the company of Miss Lucinda Bridges, an aspiring young actress. The columnist said that while Gathen Bentley was on tour, the blond beauty had busied herself by appearing in a Broadway play that was mildly pleasing, according to the columnist.

There was even a photograph of them. She was holding on to his arm and the camera caught them just as she looked up to speak to him, and he looked down smiling at her.

The pain was too severe to bring even one tear. She

gazed over the hills with dry eyes and thought, "What else could I expect?"

It was becoming quite apparent that the newspapers had accepted Arthur's death as accidental and would not pursue it any further.

One day, Anais approached Tillie with the idea of going back to New York.

"I think it's time," Tillie said. Even though she desperately wanted to go back to New York, Tillie would not have dreamed of going back if it would in some way cause emotional harm to Andy, and she would never have left Anais alone. But she was happy that the time was right to go back.

Adelaide came to spend the entire day with Anais the last week that they were at Gathen's, and they spent the day horseback riding.

Spring had just arrived and the woods were sweet with the fragrance of budding trees that were just beginning to spread colors of pale delicate green to a dark and drab landscape, and tender white violets bloomed in the meadows.

They dismounted from their horses and walked them along a rushing stream that showered over rocks into a little waterfall.

"It's so beautiful here," Adelaide said, drawing in a deep breath, taking in all the beauty that surrounded her.

"It is," Anais agreed. "I just hope that I never have to use it as a hideout again." Adelaide took note of the bitterness in Anais' calm and brittle voice.

"I don't think that you will. It's over, Anais. Let the

memory die," she said. She examined Anais' face carefully, trying to see how much this suffering had damaged her. It had left its mark, but Adelaide was sure that it would be worn with grace, and after a while no one would ever know that it was there but it would always be there.

"I worry so about Andy," Anais said.

"If you are worrying because Arthur was his father, we are all individuals and we make our own choices in this world. Regardless of our circumstances, each of us is held accountable for our own deeds."

Adelaide was studying Anais' face and she said, "I met Arthur's father when he came up to school, and I have never met a kinder nor prouder man in my life. I see him in Andy." She blew out a breath of exasperation. "I think Arthur was a freak, and so was Elliott; thank heavens you never married him. It happens. If you think about it, who ever heard of anyone else in Hitler's family?" Anais smiled at Adelaide and her moment of wisdom.

"That's true. I don't see anything of Arthur in Andy, and in all honesty, Andy hardly knew him. Arthur was too busy making his mark." She shook her head sadly. "Do you know Andy hasn't asked very much about Arthur? He knows that he was killed in a plane crash, and for now that's enough. Later, much later, we'll see what more he will need to know." Anais' voice trailed off. Then she said, "What troubles me is that Julia married a man that didn't even like her. Now we know why she seemed so changed before . . . the accident."

Anais looked out over the meadows and said, "It's all been made up to her now. Julia can be at peace, and that's good." She looked sad. "And as for Elliott, I'm only disappointed in him as a person. I was no longer in love with him."

"Have you heard from Gathen?" Adelaide ventured to ask.

"No, not a word, but I did see him with Miss Bridges in one of the New York newspapers." Anais' faint smile was filled with sadness.

"I hardly think that that means anything," Adelaide said defensively.

"They looked rather happy to me," Anais said.

"When a person falls in love, they might fall very quickly, but they don't fall out of love that easily," Adelaide continued her argument.

"All it takes is one special person, and everything else is forgotten," Anais replied.

"Well, we'll see about that, won't we?" Adelaide had had enough of the conversation. She took the rein of her horse and said, "Come, let's get back. Tillie's probably chafing at the bit to get back to New York."

The house on Sutton Place stood lonely and silent. There had been no one there since January except for Robert, who looked after the place, but when Anais unlocked the door, the house came to life. There were flowers everywhere and her mother and father were waiting in the living room.

"Welcome home, darling," her mother said, and Andy ran to his grandfather's open arms.

"Oh, I'm so glad that you're here," Anais cried.

"Well, Tillie, I think everything is all right, and we

want to thank you from the bottom of our hearts," Anais' father said warmly to Tillie.

"I'm glad it's over," Tillie said.

"Amen to that," Anais' father said, "but I think we came through it well. No one looks the worse for wear, and I think country air sort of agrees with you," he said teasingly.

"Well, thank you very much, but I think I'm going to stick with the soot and fumes," Tillie replied with a scoff.

Robert brought in some coffee and little sandwiches and they began to fill each other in on the latest news. Nothing had taken place since the memorial. Everything had remained quiet and routine. They were just a family adjusting to the death of one of its members, which was of no great interest to the general public.

After Andy had left the room, Anais asked her father who had been in the cottage the morning she and Tillie had done some investigating of their own.

"When you were at the house just before Thanksgiving, it was Streicher. Arthur and Elliott had taken him up there after you accidentally met them on the street. It was much more isolated and it was highly dangerous for Streicher to be in this country, and you sort of messed things up for them when you went up to the house earlier than usual. Arthur and Elliott had put him into the cottage, and I suppose when he turned the light on there was a crack in the drapes. He probably saw it, but little flares of light travel far when there is nothing but darkness around, and it was too late. You had seen it for just a brief second and that was enough to send you and Karl down to investigate."

Her father paused for a moment. "This has been the damnedest thing. I suppose they got him out of there during the night."

"But what about the morning Tillie and I went to the cottage and found the stove warm? Someone must have been there again," she said.

"Yes, you seemed to have had a way of getting into everyone's way." Her father laughed.

"You know that you have taught me to question everything that I didn't understand," Anais chided her father.

"I'm going to have to reevaluate my own theory. I have a wife who doesn't knock on doors, and a daughter whose curiosity is overbearing. Anyway, when we figured out what the hell was going on with Arthur." Her father stopped for a moment. "Funny, we didn't figure Elliott in this. And I'm truly sorry, honey."

Anais made a small gesture with her hands and she could only say, "Well," but that was water under the bridge as far as she was concerned.

"Getting back to Arthur," her father continued, "E.B. flew up to Washington on his way here to consult with the Agency. They sent some of their agents up and found out exactly what was going on, and from a double agent in Paraguay, they found out exactly when they planned to kidnap Andy."

At this point her father stopped and rubbed his knees, and for a moment age crept across his handsome face.

"I'll tell you, these men have dealt with every kind of treachery you can think of, and even they were shocked that a man would plot to kidnap his own son for ransom."

Anais' mother got up and walked to the window. Even

though it was over, she found that she could still be shaken at the mention of Arthur's plot.

"And I will tell you that they would have gotten every cent they wanted." Her father too could still be shaken, Anais saw, by recounting the story, and his voice cracked.

"Of course, you know that Arthur would have been the aggrieved father, doing everything possible to have his son returned safely. That son of a—" Her father remembered the ladies and let the unfinished word hang in the air.

Anais' mother spoke: "There's no need to say that we will ever forget this, but for the moment, there's no need for Andy to know any of it, and, if he has to know later on in life, so be it. I think that there will have been enough love for him in this family to allow him to handle anything that will come."

She gazed tenderly at Tillie and said to her, "And you know, Tillie, that you are as much a part of this family as any member. Heaven only knows you've been as much mother to Anais as I have, with me taking a back seat at times." She and Tillie smiled warmly at each other and Tillie said, "I for one don't think this family has anything to worry about. And I've always had a gut feeling about Arthur and Elliott. I've never liked either of them; too . . . proper. If you know what I mean."

"I think I do," Anais' mother said.

"Getting back to you two lady detectives," Anais' father interrupted, "the morning you and Tillie went down to the cottage, the agents saw you coming and had to scramble out of there, using branches to dust away their tracks, and it was snowing hard enough to cover the marks of the branches before you got there. They were always on the watch, and only used the cottage to warm up during their breaks."

"I knew those men weren't from the sheriff's office," Anais said.

"Well," her father said, "they got von Stressmann, or whatever his name was. They won't be looking for him anymore."

Anais' eyes flickered. That would mean that they had known that the plane was to go down. But she chose not to question her father any further. If she did not know for certain it would be much easier to pretend that the plane had gone down due to bad weather, but she suddenly lost her appetite for the little sandwiches; she glanced at her mother and Tillie and they both still seemed to have been relishing their food, so Anais knew that they had missed this clue, and her father did not realize that he had let anything slip.

Anais stretched and said, "It's spring and we will soon be going back to Italy."

"Yes," her mother said, "and we will take the summer to forget as much as possible."

Tillie rolled her eyes to the ceiling and said, "Here we go again."

"Tillie, why don't you come to Rome with us for a rest?" Anais asked.

"No, I'm going to let you go to Rome for a rest. I'm going to stay right here and miss all of you, in a very pleasant way." Tillie nodded her head to affirm her statement. They all laughed.

After her parents left with Andy, things seemed to be getting back to normal; the house was suddenly quiet.

Tillie was back in her own domain and had gone happily off to her kitchen to see what harm had been done in her absence.

Anais stood at the French doors watching the river flow by, which at times seemed the only place to quiet a troubled mind, as sometimes the flickering flames in a fireplace did. She tried desperately to sort out the things that were troubling her, and it was no use: she was just lonely. There were no urgent matters to occupy her thoughts now. She would now have time to think and to regret, and to fill her mind with the what-ifs, and what in the world was she going to do with her life?

A week had passed since Anais arrived back in the city. She had tried to resume her life as it had been, but she found herself listless and disinclined to take part in things that had once interested her. She was sitting in her room watching the river, as she so often did lately. The telephone rang and she turned from her solitary vigilance of the rushing East River.

Her voice was subdued as she answered the phone. It was Adelaide. While not subdued at all, Adelaide did not speak in her usual vivacious tone.

"Anais, I must go up to the country. I was wondering if you might like to drive up with me."

"Oh, I don't know, Adelaide." Anais heaved a sigh of unhappiness.

"Come, Anais. I don't really feel like driving up alone."

"Is Gathen back?" Anais asked.

"Why, I don't know. Why do you ask?" Adelaide paused.

"I left some things there. I can pick them up and take them to our house," Anais said.

"Then I'll pick you up at nine in the morning."

Anais hung up the phone and thought that it best to have all the LaPrell things out of Gathen's house before he returned, and this was a good time to do that. She would have Adelaide for support.

Anais was waiting on the steps when Adelaide pulled up to the curb in her silver Rolls-Royce. As always, Adelaide looked in perfect character. Her dark hair was pulled back and caught with a silk scarf; a beige cashmere sweater was draped around her shoulders. She reached over the seat and opened the door for Anais.

"Who would want to spend a day like today in the city?" she said, settling herself again behind the wheel.

It was ten-thirty when they turned in to the long driveway that led to Gathen's house.

"I won't be a moment," Anais said, getting out of the car. "And I can see if Bessie has put everything in order."

They walked around the back of the house, where the breathtaking view now showed delicate pale-green leaves sprouting over everything; white and pink blossoms quivered on dark branches that were flowing with new sap; a gentle breeze sent a shower of pink petals floating noiselessly on the soft April wind.

Anais did not see Adelaide turn and go up the stone steps to the terrace. She strode down the hill, breathing in the beautiful April morning. She wanted to look closer at the cherry tree that was spraying the air and the ground without a whisper.

Suddenly a man appeared through the trees. Anais

stopped in her tracks. She had the greatest urge to turn and run or try to hide someplace, but she stood in open space and there was nowhere for her to go.

"Gathen, I didn't realize that you were back," she stammered, which made her feel even more foolish. "I was just going to see if everything was in order for you."

"Everything is fine," he said.

"I'm glad." She drew in a deep breath, trying to think of something else pleasant to say, but Gathen was making it very difficult for her.

"I'm back to stay, Anais." She looked at him with a questioning look.

"Have I given you enough time to clear all the doubts that were in your mind?"

"Oh, Gathen," she said finally understanding what he was getting to.

"I've stepped aside once, I won't step aside again." She watched him through misty eyes, and she saw the eyes that beheld her; eyes that less than a year ago sparkled with youth and innocence, now looked upon her with the burning desire of manhood, and they were deeply focused on what he was proclaiming as his and would never relinquish. He lifted her face in his hands and brushed aside a cherry blossom that had caught in her hair and smiled down at her. The softness of love had replaced the demand that had burned in his eyes only a moment ago.

"I was not going to marry Elliott. I couldn't," she said through tears.

"I know. I was just waiting." He laughed. "We belonged to each other from the very first moment. Weren't we lucky?"

"Oh, yes, darling." She cried in his arms and he tenderly kissed her.

From the terrace Adelaide and Wells could see their passionate embrace.

"Thank God," Adelaide whispered.

Anais had surrendered to the happiness that awaited her in Gathen's arms.